MW00877485

Secrets in the Land of Cheese

Katiera Pfeister

CreateSpace Independent Publishing Platform,
North Charleston, SC

Copyright © 2015 by Katiera Pfeister

All rights reserved.

ISBN:1508752931

ISBN-13:978-1508752936

BISAC: Juvenile Fiction / Religious / Christian / Mysteries & Detective
Stories

Library of Congress Control Number: 2015904161

CreateSpace Independent Publishing Platform,
North Charleston, SC

Scripture quotations marked (NIV) taken from the HOLY BIBLE, NEW
INTERNATIONAL VERSION, Copyright 1973, 1978, 1984 International
Bible Society.

Scripture quotations marked (NLT) are taken from the Holy Bible, New
Living Translation, copyright © 1996, 2004, 2007 by Tyndale House
Foundation. Used by permission of Tyndale House Publishers, Inc., Carol
Stream, Illinois 60188. All rights reserved.

For information regarding permission to use this material for
any purpose write to **katiera.pfeister@yahoo.com**

DEDICATION

This book is dedicated to The One who
Created this World and took the punishment
for the sins of all mankind. The One who
calls us to be close to Him.
And, to my husband, Jeremy. I love living life with
you. You are a gift from God.
You both hold my heart.

Chapter 1

CHEESE SODAVILLE

"Follow me," the vice principal said as she led me quickly down the hall. The town was so small, there was only one school building for everyone. The sign on the way in read: *Welcome to Hillcrest, Wisconsin. The Home of Delicious Cheese Soda, Population 930.*

"The sixth grade classroom is right here," the vice principal said, interrupting my thoughts.

"Are you okay?" She asked. "You look a little pale."

"Yes. I'm okay. I always look pale." It was true. I was Magdelan, the girl who looked like she had never seen the sun. Why couldn't my parents have moved to Florida where I could have finally gotten a tan?

"Well, maybe it's just that pretty dark hair that makes you look pale." She gave me a reassuring pat on the shoulder as a loud squeal came from down the hall.

"You've got to be kidding!" the nice lady seemed to forget about me. She turned and stomped toward a boy wearing overalls. He was carrying something that looked like a pig.

"Wilmer, you get back here at once!" Insisted the vice principal. As she disappeared, I felt a moment of relief, a moment all to myself.

One look at my ankles told me my jeans were still tight-rolled. I took a deep breath and peered through the small window in the classroom door. The teacher spotted me right away and waved me in.

"Class, we have a new student today. Her name is Magdelan Pierce. Magdelan, I heard you might like to be called Maggie."

I nodded.

"You can hang your *beg* on one of those empty hooks."

My eyebrows wrinkled in confusion. "Right *heeere*" Mrs. Hebner spoke slowly with a look of concern as she pulled my backpack from my hand and hung it on an open hook.

"Oh, my bag!" I uttered, quickly turning to find the empty desk she was pointing toward.

I sat up straight, ran my fingers through my dark brown waves, opened the math book on my desk and forced my mind to focus on the words coming out of my new teacher's mouth.

The morning was a blur. My new teacher covered everything from finding the mean of a set of numbers to the settling of Jamestown, all in three hours. I felt like saying, "Slow down." But, I could already tell that Mrs. Hebner was not only fast-paced, she was no-nonsense.

There wasn't time to get to know anyone but I did look around a little. Next to me sat a cute, blond-haired girl who seemed friendly. She smiled every time I looked her way. Her name was Kadie Brady, and I figured we would be friends. On my other side was a boy named Scott. He seemed nice, but kept looking at me with what I called "the sneaky smile"—a smile that said, "I know you think I'm cute." Whenever I saw that smile, the stubborn side of me thought, "I'm going to refuse to let you know I think you're cute."

Another girl named Crystal had a pretty face and deep, blue eyes, but what stood out was her hair. It was blond and very short. She had it spiked on top with a tail in the back. I had never—not even in pictures—seen a girl with a haircut like this. I was definitely curious about Crystal.

"All right class, put away your things. It's time to get ready for the lunch bell," instructed Mrs. Hebner. "Who would like to help Magdelan find the *bubbler* and the bathroom?"

To my relief, Kadie raised her hand.

The bubbler was a drinking fountain. On our way to lunch, Kadie filled me in on all kinds of important sixth-grade news. I met Robby, whose hair was as orange as pumpkin pie. Michelle munched on a Milky Way bar and waved as Kadie introduced us. Kadie whispered, "No one ever sees Michelle eat anything but candy."

I walked by a girl named Bonnie without saying hello because she was giving me a, "let's-have-a-duel-at-sundown" kind of look. I knew that look all too well. It was the same look Malia Watson had given me in third grade; the day she hid behind a tree and jumped out to beat me up on the way home from school.

I decided to keep an eye on Bonnie but refused to let her ruin my day. I might have been a little on the scrawny side but she didn't look nearly as strong as Malia.

Lunch was delicious. Since there weren't many students, the school served homemade food. Michelle was really missing out. I learned that Kadie and a boy named Davey both lived on dairy farms. There were 16 sixth graders altogether, and I had the feeling that most of them had known each other since before they had teeth.

As Mrs. Hebner came in to pick us up from lunch, she asked, "What did you eat for lunch, Michelle?"

Michelle winced and didn't answer.

Mrs. Hebner shook her head and continued, "How do you expect to grow if you eat nothing but candy. Your bones need calcium."

"I had a cheese soda." Michelle threw in as if she thought it would impress the teacher.

What is cheese soda? I wondered. It didn't sound like a very good idea.

Gym class was where the day started to go downhill. Gym at my old school was a slightly more organized recess. We ran relays, played dodge ball, or messed around with a parachute. The truth was, unless you counted kickball, I had never come close to playing a single organized sport.

So, it was pretty scary when the gym teacher announced we were choosing teams for a basketball relay. Our instructions were to dribble the ball across the length of the gym, make a basket, dribble back, and pass the ball to the next person. The gym teacher, Mr. Martin, made it sound easy.

I stood in the back of the line with jittery legs. I noticed most of the students were basketball superstars. The line moved fast, and suddenly it was my turn. My team was in the lead, so the kids were yelling for me to hurry.

I muttered a desperate, "I like to watch basketball, but I don't know how to play." I'm pretty sure no one heard me, but it didn't take long for them to notice.

I dribbled like a five-year-old. When I finally made it to the basket, I took the leather ball into my hands and heard it laughing at me. It said, "You can't get me in the basket. I'm going to do whatever I want."

I heaved the ball in the general direction of the rim, but it hit the bottom of the backboard. I heard groans behind me. My team didn't have a chance. On my third try, I resorted to a granny throw. That was when I heard the other team cheer. Knowing they had won, I hoped it was all over, but was afraid to look behind me.

As I prepared for another shot, Mr. Martin approached, showing me how to hold the ball. Still, my next five throws barely hit the bottom of the backboard. My last throw slammed into the post and came back to hit me in the shoulder.

My face felt hot, and I knew it was bright red. I was just thankful I was able to hold back my tears of embarrassment. I could tell Mr. Martin was not the kind of guy who let just anyone quit, but I was thankful he made an exception for me. The last words of gym class made me shudder. Mr. Martin said, "Okay, we'll practice that again tomorrow."

On the bus ride home, my sisters and I crowded into the same seat and shared stories about our first day of school.

"Did your teacher call the drinking fountain a bubbler?" Carrie giggled.

"Yes, and she called my bag a *'beg'*," I added. "I was like, 'What are you talking about?"

"And everyone talks about cheese like it's candy or something." Bernice nodded as we all laughed at our new home.

None of us wanted to move away from Battle Creek. We were extremely attached to our family and our friends. We begged our parents to stay—up to the day the movers came to pack the furniture and everything else we owned into a huge truck.

During the seven hour drive to Hillcrest I realized that each step of moving was kind of like taking off an enormous Band-Aid. It was scary, but after I finally gave in and ripped it off, it was not as awful as I thought it would be. Instead, I was relieved that life went on.

Our new house was better than our old one. We loved it the moment we saw it. It felt like it had been frozen in time because no one had lived in it since 1960. Mom said the bright walls and checkered kitchen floor made it a retro style house. The Realtor didn't know why it was empty for so long but once we saw it we didn't ask any questions.

My parents had their own bathroom attached to their room in the new house. Carrie and I each had our own room. Six-year old Bernice and three-year-old Tilly shared a room upstairs. Annika's crib was in the small room next to my parents' bedroom. It fit our family perfectly!

The basement and yard were the best parts. The basement floor was covered in mismatched tiles from all over the world. There were tiles with beautiful paintings and tiles written in so many different languages. In the back corner, we had found a surprise pile of old board games left by the previous owner. The yard was a one-acre hill speckled with big trees. At the bottom of the hill was a lake; on the other side of the lake was the main part of town. It was an amazing view!

When we got home from school, Mom offered us pretzels with our first taste of the famous Hill's Cheese Soda. We took turns telling her our stories. When I got to the part about the basketball game, I started to freak out. The worst part of it all, the part that made this almost unbearable, was I had to go back to school and do it all over again.

Mom said, "It'll be okay. You may be surprised at how quickly you learn to play basketball."

"No mom! I stink!" I tried to convince her of the seriousness of the situation as I took my first sip of the disgusting pop. "Everyone was staring at me and I could not get the ball into the basket!"

"Do you stink as bad as cheese flavored pop?" asked Carrie with a mischievous smile on her face.

I decided to ignore her.

"Time to get to work," Mom announced when she saw we had finished our pretzels.

I took my second swig of cheese soda without thinking as I dragged myself off the stool. The thought of playing basketball again was so disturbing I hardly noticed the taste. It was like a block of sharp cheddar that had been rotting in someone's car for a week.

Chapter 2

I CAN BE BRAVE

For God has not given us a spirit of fear and timidity,
but of power, love, and self-discipline.
2 Timothy 1:7 (NLT)

The night was busy. My sisters and I wanted to
keep exploring the basement, but there was no time.
We threw together macaroni and cheese with hot dogs,
unpacked a few boxes, and it was time for bed. As I lay
still, I could faintly hear my mom and dad talking.

I closed my eyes and tried to turn off my brain
for the night, but my thoughts continued to whirl
around me. They filled the room with doubts and
questions. I tried to battle the dread that kept creeping
into my brain, but I could tell I was about to lose this
familiar fight.

When I was in kindergarten, I had a fear of witches. It started when Willy Jones, who was kind of a bully, tried to scare all of the girls in my class by telling us his mom was a witch who turned into a bat every night. He said she flew around, casting evil spells on girls he didn't like. My dad had already killed two bats in our house. Within a week, a bat flew into the room that Carrie and I shared. From then on, I was sure there were witches in my room every night. I would lie in bed staring at the window, afraid to close my eyes. Now, I could see how that particular fear was totally loony.

The next big fear came in third grade. I watched the movie "Jaws" and, for the next year, I couldn't swim in a lake or pool without imagining a shark following me, ready to bite off my leg. I would even take a peek into the toilet several times before sitting down because in my imagination there was a shark waiting to bite me in the butt. Now, I can see this fear was also insane.

Lately, a completely new fear had taken over. I didn't know where it came from. While I was lying in bed, I imagined my family had left the oven on and our house was going to catch on fire while we were sleeping. I was getting up several times to check the oven dial and make sure it was turned off. I repeatedly climbed into bed, asking myself questions like, "Are you sure the oven is off?" I was sure that someday I would look back on this fear and realize it was just as crazy as the others. For now, I felt responsible for keeping my family safe from the fire in my imagination.

I couldn't sleep. I grabbed my flashlight and moved slowly toward my book box in the closet. On my way, I noticed places where the curtains were not completely closed. I quickly tried to stretch them over the corners. It was a creepy night. As I opened the closet door, my senses were aware of every creak. I gave the whole closet a close look to make sure nothing creepy was hiding in the corners when I noticed a deep looking gap between two floorboards. When I shined the light toward the gap, it looked like something colorful was under the floor.

I reached down to jiggle the floorboard and felt it move to reveal what looked like a hole.

Slowly, I crept to the kitchen to grab something I could use for prying.

In the kitchen, I noticed the microwave clock read *11:30*. "Ugh!" I checked the knobs on the stove carefully then quickly found the silverware drawer and a butter knife. Whatever might be in the slot was going to be my secret, so I cautiously tiptoed back to my room.

Now, I felt a much better kind of fear, an excited fear that I could push through because I was sure there were diamonds or gold coins under the floor. I slid the knife into the wooden slit easily and jiggled it until the panel loosened. A layer of sticky dust loosened with it.

As adrenaline pumped through my hands; I used the knife like a crow bar and lifted the wood on each side until it popped. I saw a hole that looked like it might be deep. My light shined into the recesses of the small space, but all I could see was a pile of neatly stacked envelopes wrapped in a dried yellow ribbon. *Bummer, I was hoping for treasure.*

I reached in carefully to grab the entire stack and the ribbon cracked open in my hands. The envelopes felt so dry and brittle. I closed the opening in the closet and hopped into bed.

All of the letters were to someone named Arne Werfel. Every one of them was sent to the address of our new house. Most of the letters were from Cecelia Walsh. Some, were sent from the United States and had fancy three-cent stamps; several were sent from Germany. A few were from Agatha or Detlef Werfel. It might not have been treasure, but it was mysterious. I decided to open the letters from Cecelia first.

Dear Mr. Werfel,   *August 2, 1958*

You are a special man, and I am glad to be working with you. You have treated me with great respect, and you have listened to my ideas in the shop, which makes me very happy. I like to hear your stories about Germany and would love to go there someday and see the people and places for myself. I am already learning German faster than anyone else in my class at the university, and my teacher says I may be chosen to study in Germany next year. I know I owe it to you and your friendship. May we always be friends.

Sincerely, Cecelia

Dear Arne,   *February 23, 1959*

I want you to know how much I care for you. It's not only because you make irresistible cheese strudel. It's because you understand me.

Sincerely, Cecelia

Cecelia and Arne sounded like such nice people. These were almost starting to sound like love letters.

Dear Arne,   *4 October, 1959*

Germany is the way you described it. The people are trying hard to resolve the painful past, and they are working for a better future. The family I am staying with is nice, and the food is, of course, delicious. I am mostly speaking German now, and I understand most of what the people say. Everyone seems to have a different idea about what Germany needs, and I'm wondering which way will work best in the end. I have been invited to many different meetings on campus to talk about politics, and I find the meetings to be interesting.

Sincerely, Cecelia

Dear Arne,   *October 17, 1959*

Can you believe I met your brother yesterday? He was visiting from East Germany and we met in a bakery by chance. I was in a bakery because I miss you. He must miss you too. I saw the name on his uniform and asked if he was your brother and he was. Your brother reminds me of you, but he is more regal and a little scary. I didn't know you came from such an influential family. He said you have forgotten your family. I told him you have not forgotten them at all.

Sincerely, Cecelia

This was getting a little interesting.

Dear Arne,   *January 17, 1960*

I am sorry I have not written for a while. I have been busy with school and now I am preparing to return to the United States. I will miss Germany, but I am ready to be home. I will be continuing at the University of Wisconsin in the spring. As I think about graduating, I have many important decisions to make.

Mit freundlichen Gruessen, Cecelia

Dear Arne,   *April 25, 1960*

Meet me tonight in our canoe spot by the lake. I want to talk to you.

Cecelia

P.S. 0-14-018724-3 p 204 Johanna's mother

Now the year was 1988. These letters were 30 years old! Whatever happened to Arne and Cecelia? I wondered if they got married and lived in this house. For now, I had to sleep.

Chapter 3

Deal with it and Do Better Next Time

If your boss is angry at you, don't quit!
A quiet spirit can overcome even great mistakes.
Ecclesiastes 10:4 (NLT)

Before I knew it, there was sunlight shining against my eyelids. I rolled over to hide. It was only my second day of school and I was a complete mess. I rolled out of bed and plopped on the floor. After a quick look through my closet, I decided to wear jeans and a Detroit Pistons tee shirt.

As I fully awoke from my fog, I remembered that today the basketball embarrassment would continue. My mom informed me that I looked like I had slept in the garage. I moaned and groaned all through breakfast but she still made me get on the bus.

When I got to class, the first thing Mrs. Hebner said was, "please take out your homework and pass it to the front of the room."

No! I remembered her saying something about homework, but it was all a blur.

I watched in desperation, as Mrs. Hebner collected the papers students passed to the front of the class. She eyed us all carefully and looked at the pile as if she knew exactly how thick it should be.

"Magdelan, did you do your homework?" she inquired, flipping through the pages.

I had nothing to say except, "No, I'm sorry. I haven't unpacked my pencils yet."

Obviously annoyed with this pathetic answer, I watched her consider which form of torture would work best on me. It took her just a few seconds to decide,"Sit on the bench at recess, and tomorrow I want to see your vocabulary definitions and a sentence for each one."

My punishment could have been worse, but I was now the homework forgetting, bad basketball playing new girl. I wanted to yell, "give me a break people, I just moved here." Thankfully, I kept my composure.

When it came time for gym class, I changed into my red gym shorts and took a quick look in the locker room mirror. I stunk at basketball, but I looked a little cuter in my gym outfit than expected. I stepped into the gym with hesitant determination.

"Your name is Maggie right?" I heard Bonnie ask behind me.

"Yes, and isn't your name Bonnie?" I turned and tried to smile.

"I love your name. Psych" she laughed and flicked her dangly earrings. "It's just a little hard for me to get used to a Maggie person. The only Maggie's I know are dogs," and she strutted away.

I shrugged and moved forward to begin my warm-up run. Maybe if I had slept more than six hours I would have cared.

Mr. Martin blew the whistle and the class lined up to wait for team assignments. Scott and Christy were the captains. I took one step backward; to let them know I was okay with the fact that no one was going to pick me.

To my complete surprise, the first name I heard was, "Maggie." I stayed back for a moment, expecting to hear. "Psych!" but, after a few seconds I stepped forward reluctantly. There was no comeback.

The teacher probably made them pick me first, but I didn't care. I knew now, that this basketball relay was not such a big deal. After ten tries, I finally made my first basket. Of course, my team lost again, but I was over my first major obstacle of sixth grade.

I headed home on the bus, still feeling liberated. Carrie and Bernice were sitting with new friends and I was on my own, but I didn't mind. The day turned out to be so much better than expected.

As we walked in the door, I noticed the house was starting to look like home. I saw the familiar furniture and wall decorations from our old house. They seemed to fit very well in Wisconsin. One of my favorites was my dad's painting of the dancing girls. It looked like a fairy tale. There were five willow trees whose long, wispy branches spread out mixing with the girls' arms so you couldn't tell where the tree ended and the girls began.

Mom was in the kitchen sitting at one of the new bar stools. She looked pleased with her day and remembered to ask about the basketball game. I was happy to report, it went better than I ever imagined. I still stunk at basketball, but at least I might have some new friends.

My sisters and I finally explored the basement were we each claimed our favorite tile. I wondered how many of the tiles were from Germany as I chose a brown tile with a colorful painting of the earth as my favorite.

By bedtime I had just enough energy to pull out my flashlight and read the other letters. All of them were from Germany with German addresses and German postage.

Liebe Sohn,

Ihr Vater und ich hart gearbeitet, um ihnen ein gutes Leben. Ich hoffe, sie werden nicht vergessen.

Deine Mutter

I shook my head and mindlessly tossed the letter over my shoulder, I didn't know one word of German. This was useless to me.

Arne   *6 June 1951*

You have betrayed your friends and your own family, and I cannot simply forgive and forget. Mother begins to cry every time your name is mentioned. East Germany may not be what we wish it were, but it is still our home. The Stasi serves to keep it that way. To leave Germany is to wish you had never known her.

When you write to mother, please keep it brief and cordial, but do not pretend to have any loyalty to your family. You are a traitor. I would write to you in German, but I fear you may have forgotten your mother tongue.

With regret,

Detlef

Arne   *1 April 1960*

Mother has died and with her passing I find no reason to communicate with you. I will be taking a wife and moving into the family estate during the coming months. My plan is to forget I ever had a brother.

Detlef

This Detlef guy sounded like an awful brother. Had Arne really done something terrible or was Detlef a drama queen? I wondered how I could find out more about Arne Werfel without telling anyone about these letters. I hid all of the letters in my backpack hoping for a chance to learn more.

On Saturday, our dad liked to wake us up around 8am. He would say something like, "stop wasting the day away and get out of bed." Then, he would cut wood, mow the lawn or fix things outside until lunch, while Mom, my sisters, and I each picked slips of rolled up paper with jobs listed on them out of my mom's basket of chores. It didn't matter what house we lived in, this was the routine. After each chore, Mom played a card game while we all took a short break. Then we would pick another job. It was very effective, but after years of picking jobs, we felt the need to complain. Our whining never worked, Mom lived in her own world where her little basket of jobs was a basket of fun.

My last job on Saturday was to feed Annika her mushy peas and pears, "*Vroom-Vroom*, open the hatch, the airplane is coming." I announced as I carefully spooned the food into her mouth. Half of it did go down the hatch, but half of it got in her hair and on her bib. I even found a bit of mushy peas on the toaster while I was cleaning up.

Mom had heard from the neighbors that the fishing lake behind our house was not good for swimming after all. The rumor was that even though it's illegal, one of the families on the block pumped all of their sewage into the lake. At first I didn't believe the rumor. I mean, who would pump everything from their toilet into a beautiful lake? But then, Carrie and I put on our shorts and decided to do some exploring of our own. As we took our first step, our feet literally sunk two feet down into muck, until we were up to our knees in goop. We imagined our feet sinking deep into a lake of poop. It was so bad; we had to get Dad's help to pull us out of the lake.

The lake was pretty to look at though and there was an old looking canoe left in the garage. After a few repairs, Dad said it was ready for a test run. Mom and Dad rowed across the lake and back without spotting any leaks.

They handed us the oars, we put on our life jackets, and Dad gave us a push. What were they thinking?

We awkwardly rowed the boat out to the middle of the lake and turned to wave to everyone. I leaned my paddle against my lap while I waved excitedly with both hands.

Not a good idea. Before I could reach for it, into the lake dropped my paddle. As soon as the paddle hit the water it started floating away. I stretched my body as far as I could without falling into the water, but could not reach the paddle.

"Oops!" was all I could think to say as I looked back at my parents to see if they had noticed my mistake.

"What'd ya do?" Carrie could hardly believe her eyes.

"I dropped it!" I squealed as we both let out nervous giggles.

Carrie grabbed her paddle firmly and moved it through the water. Her effort was useless. The canoe glided in a perfect circle.

"Oh great, how are we gonna get back home?" Carrie eyed me blamefully.

I winced and shrugged my shoulders, because I didn't have a single idea. Carrie continued to paddle for three or four more minutes while I leaned to one side to help the canoe move forward.

After a few minutes of this, my parents noticed we were having problems. Carrie held up her paddle and I held up my empty hands until they figured it out. I could see their frustrated faces. I had stuck them with quite a problem.

The neighbors, with the really fancy house had a rowboat and after an hour, when the sun was setting, the paddle had drifted to their shore where Dad retrieved it. A man approached dad and they talked briefly before climbing into a boat. The sky was beautiful behind the boat's shadowy figure as it came closer. At last we could see Dad and the man, clearly.

"So you dropped your paddle in the water did ya?" the man called as he floated toward us.

I apologized and thanked them both, knowing my dad hated to inconvenience anyone. Dad introduced us to our rescuer, Dr. Morrison, who was a college professor. "Did you know your new house has quite a story?" Dr. Morrison asked.

"No, we know it's been empty since the sixties," my dad answered.

"The man who owned your house last, came to

the United States as a German World War 2 refugee. He must have traded secrets for a chance at a new life in the states. When I moved to Hillcrest ten years ago, I soon learned about Arne who owned a bakery in town. But then, he was charged with murder thirty years ago, and he's been in prison ever since. The woman's body was never found. More than a few people think her bones are in this lake."

"Wow, that's quite a story!" Dad's eyes opened wide.

I *gulped*.

"*Whoa*! I think I see her bones" Carrie whispered to me and pointed at some seaweed.

We all peered down into the quiet water. First poop, now bones. What else was down there?

Could it be true? Could the nice man from the letters be a murderer? I didn't want to believe it.

The next morning we visited a church ten miles away in Beaverdam. Carrie and I liked our Sunday school class and the pastor's sermon kept my attention. He preached about 1 Peter 5 and when he read verse seven, I was all ears. I followed along as he read, "Give all of your cares to God, because He cares for you." The pastor explained that God wants to hear about our troubles and our fears. He said that as we talk to God, He helps us in ways that we can't even imagine. I already knew God loved me, but I had never thought about telling Him my weird fears. I wondered if He would think I was crazy.

During the next week I gave it a try. I tried talking to The Great Maker of the World about what was on my mind. I talked to Him about the oven, the letters, Bonnie, and my ongoing failures. The amazing thing was that it really seemed like He was with me. He was helping me sleep, helping me make friends and even helping me to remember to do my homework.

On Friday night, Kadie had a birthday party. During the party, I played my first game of Truth or Dare. Everything about the game was pure fun. When my turn came, Lena, the girl I just met, asked, "Truth or Dare" and I chose Dare. My challenge was to knock on Kadie's older brother's door and when he opened the door, I was supposed to say, "Here are your underwear," and hand him his pile of laundry. Kadie's brother was cute, but on this particular night my only goal was to have fun with the girls. I had to do it!

Everyone giggled as I knocked on the door and

waited for him to come. I knocked a second time and he opened the door, obviously annoyed.

Then, to my surprise, I had one of those rare moments when I found my funny. I looked him in the eye and said in a sweet voice, "Here are your undies." He rolled his eyes and grabbed the pile as we all ran away squealing.

The rest of the night, all eight of us girls laughed non-stop. The night got even funnier when Michelle popped up talking in her sleep and begging "Mom- I want to learn ballet. I want to dance on the stage." I was sure she was faking, but she never cracked a smile. Maybe it was a side effect of the unbelievable amount of Skittles that girl could scarf.

At breakfast, I asked everyone if they had heard of anyone named Arne Werfel. I didn't want to believe what the neighbor had said. Could the Arne from the letters be a murderer? Kadie said the name sounded familiar, but no one seemed to know him.

"Was there ever a bakery in Hillcrest," I tried again.

"I think there was," Michelle said. "I wish there was now." We all agreed; Hillcrest needed a bakery.

Chapter 4

NOT GIRLY ENOUGH

"If you honor your father and mother, things will go well for you, and you will have a long life on the earth." Ephesians 6:3 (NLT)

The weekend passed quickly and Monday came way too soon. My sisters and I were getting slower every morning. Our mom had insisted we were going to miss the bus and have no way to get to school because my dad had the car at work. We proved her right when we heard the bus buzz by as we were grabbing our book bags one morning.

None of us wanted to miss school. It meant another day of Mom's chore basket. Thankfully, she had a crazy idea for getting us to school.

"Hurry up girls, I'll see if Mrs. Brown can come

over to the house for a few minutes, in case your little sisters wake up. This once, I'll try to take you across the lake in the canoe."

Our school was just across the lake and a few blocks down the road. We all laughed at the idea. It seemed really nuts.

"Let's do it!" yelled Carrie. And as my mom called Mrs. Brown, we all ran outside to get in the canoe.

"Carrie, you and I will paddle," Mom suggested as she gave us a push and hopped in with us. The lake was still and we easily made it across in a few minutes. We jumped out quickly, thinking we may be late for school.

"Don't let this happen again." said Mom as she pushed back toward our house. I walked up the small hill, past the bowling alley and gas station to school.

When we stepped inside, I was relieved to notice we weren't late. Robby, who rode the bus with us, asked, "What happened this morning?"

"We missed the bus, so my mom dropped us off in the canoe," I answered and realized it sounded kind of mysterious. I think most of the other students thought my family was rich because we lived in such a nice house on the lake. This was not true.

I was so glad I didn't miss the day. Our class got the best news of the school year. Mrs. Hebner started teaching us about ecosystems. Then she told us we'd be building terrariums in groups of four at tables in the middle of our desks. First, we would plant vines and then we'd each get a green anole, which is a lizard, to put inside. Now, if Mrs. Hebner had told us we were going to keep snakes in our terrariums I would have freaked out, but lizards are cute and snakes are disgusting. Kadie agreed. Michelle, the candy-holic, on the other hand, whined about the idea of having to touch a lizard. She kept asking irritating questions like, "Are we going to feed it bugs? Will we have to touch the bugs?"

Our group was Michelle, Kadie, Robby, the nice kid with orange hair, and me. Poor, quiet, Robby was all alone with us girls. "Okay" I said, "let's answer all of the questions about ecosystems fast. The faster we answer the questions the faster we will get our lizards."

"I don't want any nasty lizard," Michelle disagreed and turned away.

Robby said, "I've never had a lizard, but sometimes I catch toads or garter snakes and keep them in a box for a few days." Michelle did a barfing motion to show her disgust.

Kadie asked, "What do they eat?" None of us knew, so we turned our attention back to our study sheet and our science book.

"I wonder if our terrarium is going to have an actual food chain," said Kadie.

"All I know is my last school never did anything this cool."

At recess, Davey, Kadie, Kevin, and I had invented a new game. It all started with monkey bar races along the long T-shaped monkey bars. I was surprised at how fast I could go. Pretty soon, we decided to make it a tag game. The rules were simple: to stay in the game you had to stay on the monkey bars at all times. You could climb on top or do the monkey thing, but you weren't allowed to touch the ground. If you touched the ground you were automatically out. It was a grueling game. The biggest excitement was being able to keep up with the boys. We had played it for two days of recess and by the third day my palms and fingers were full of oozing, stinging, blisters.

"So, do you want to play Monkey Bar Tag today?" Davey asked as he walked by Kadie and I on the fourth day. I had already decided I was not going to play today, my hands were so sore, but my friends would think I was a wimp if I told them.

"Sure," I yelled, and ran to catch up to him. Kadie followed and before I knew it, I was "It." I caught Kadie and Kevin first. Now, I just had to catch up to Davey.

"There's no way you're going to catch me today" Davey challenged me and I picked up my speed. Davey was friendly and cute without being showy. So far, he was also surprisingly easy to talk to.

"You wanna bet?" I ignored the sharp pain in my hands and kept going. With every move, I could feel the metal peeling bigger holes into my hands, but I didn't give in to the pain. Davey climbed across the top of the bars and I reached one hand up to try to grab his ankle, but I was too late. I thrust my feet up and squeezed my body through two metal bars. This gave me a three second break, but he was quick and had almost reached the end of the bars. Now, he was at a dead end and as long as I moved quickly I would definitely catch him. I stopped two rungs short of the end and waited for him to make the next move. He stared at me and I caught a light of amusement in his dark brown eyes. The expression seemed to say more than "this is fun." It might have been a look that meant, "I like you." The look scared me a little and for a moment, I lost my nerve. I could hear Kadie cheering for me as Davey slipped by under the bars and the teacher blew her whistle to tell us recess was over.

For the next hour, I quietly processed what had happened during recess. In Battle Creek I had two main crushes. One was a kid at school who got kind of whiny and annoying after third grade. The other, more serious crush was in fourth grade. I had been friends with this boy until the crush started. Then, my feelings of friendship turned to feelings of butterflies in my stomach and I was afraid to even look at him. I didn't want that to happen with Davey.

I was clueless in the boy world. My mom was no help. Once she knew we had a crush on a boy, she teased us constantly and within two days she was talking on the phone with the boy's mom about how cute it all was. I was determined to keep my lips sealed.

At home, during dinner, Mom noticed my hands. "Magdelan, what happened to your hands," she asked with a gasp. I held out my swollen, red hands and explained that it was from the monkey bars at school.

"I have never seen monkey bars do that to someone's hands," she didn't seem to believe me. Then she gave my dad "The Look." The look said, "I'm concerned about Maggie." It was always followed by "The Other Look" that means, "We need to step in and do something about this."

By bedtime, Mom had made her plan. She decided that I was becoming a bit too tomboyish. She didn't like me wearing sporty tee shirts and jeans every day. She had decided, from then on, I would be wearing a dress to school at least once each week.

"Magdelan, you have all of those pretty dresses and you only wear them to church. You might as well wear them to school every once in a while." I tried to imagine myself winning Monkey Bar Tag in a slip and slippery shoes and I knew that it would be seriously dangerous and embarrassing.

"But Mom! Why?" I pleaded but I could tell that her mind was already made up and she had convinced my dad to agree with her. "Does Carrie have to wear a dress every week?" I fought in a snotty voice which only made things worse.

"Your sister already wears dresses to school, young lady. This is not open for discussion."

At that point, I imagine most girls my age would stop arguing and take their anger to their room. They might even slam the door. But I couldn't seem to keep my mouth shut and before I knew it, I told my mom to "just chill out," which was enough for her to send me to my room with a mouth full of liquid hand soap.

"Okay, you can spit it out," Mom yelled from the other room after a torturous minute. I tried to act cool about it, but I could feel some of the soap running down the back of my throat and I was about to gag. I walked quickly to the bathroom. *Spit, Spit*, drink cold water. *Spit, spit*, drink a little more cold water. *Spit, spit*, more soap, cold water. I walked calmly to the kitchen for a glass of milk. I just wanted to go to bed.

"Oh, Magdelan, before you go to bed, make sure you pick out a dress for tomorrow," Mom said in her sweetest voice, from the other room.

"Mom! Not tomorrow! Tomorrow is field day. I'm serious. I'm not lying. The whole school is going to be outside for almost the whole day." I knew it wouldn't work, she was unyielding tonight. She really didn't seem to care that I would be wearing my first dress on the day when my teacher had made it clear we are supposed to wear tennis shoes and shorts.

I fell asleep as I cried into my pillow. I was so excited about this boy, and field day was going to be so much fun. Why didn't she realize she was ruining it all? What was she so afraid of? Did she think I was going to give up girlhood all together?

The morning came way too quickly. I went straight to the bathroom to wash away the remnants of my tears. My eyelids were puffy and I felt completely bummed. This was worse than the basketball catastrophe. Maybe I could skip the day all together. I looked in my closet for a dress that wasn't lacy or puffy but there were none. There was only one I was willing to wear. It was a dark red sweater dress with semi puffy sleeves. I slipped it on with tights and my shiny black dress shoes and decided to eat a peaceful breakfast.

On the bus, I finally thought of the perfect way out. The only problem would be my shoes. If only I had thought of the idea sooner I could have brought my sneakers.

My plan worked and I showed up to field day

in my gym outfit, with no socks and shiny, slippery patent leather shoes. It was October, but thankfully, the day was nice and warm.

Kadie took one look at me and said what everyone else was thinking. "What are you wearing?" She'd never understand my explanation.

Bonnie pointed at me and whispered to Michelle. They smiled in amusement, and I wondered if I should have worn the dress after all.

"It's my mom; she totally wigged out last night and decided I need to wear more dresses," I tried to explain.

"On Field Day? Why would she make you wear a dress on Field Day?" Kadie was clearly baffled. I had no response. I couldn't even put the words together and figure out an explanation. None of it made a bit of sense to me.

"Let's just say my mom can be really mental sometimes," I knew it sounded snotty and ungrateful and I didn't even care.

I didn't win a single race all morning, but everyone seemed to get over my funny clothes. After lunch, Mrs. Hebner asked why I wore dress shoes on field day. I told her my mom made me wear a dress, so I put on my gym clothes.

"You'd better go put your dress back on," she pointed toward the building.

"I could go to the library for a while," I suggested.

"That sounds like a good idea," she agreed, looking a little suspicious.

I went inside to change and see what I could learn about Cecelia Walsh.

My first goal was to translate the German letter. The librarian, Mrs. Stinson was happy to let me use a dictionary that translated German words into English. It was a little tricky. It seemed like the letter was more blaming Arne for being a traitor to his family. The important thing was the German letter was written by Arne's Mom.

Next, I wanted to look at yearbooks. I thought Cecelia Walsh was a senior in high school in 1956 or 1957. So, if she lived in Hillcrest, I should be able to find her picture without a problem.

Mrs. Stinson was proud to pull out her

collection of old yearbooks. She eyed me funny while I looked. I tried to hide my excitement when I found Cecelia's picture. Even in the black and white photograph, she was stunning, with smooth straight blond hair and big bright eyes. Did she ever see Arne again after he went to prison? Were the rumors true? I had to know. I decided it was probably safe to bring up Cecelia's name.

"Mrs. Stinson," I began carefully. "Do you know this lady?"

I pointed out the picture to Mrs. Stinson and waited for her to look.

Mrs. Stinson's voice sounded sad as she explained, "That is Cecelia Walsh. She was four years older than me.

"What happened to her?" I probed.

Mrs. Stinson hesitated but continued, "She was murdered while she was a senior in college. It was so sad. No one could understand it. She was one of those girls who could have done anything she wanted with her life."

"What a sad story." I gasped. There were so many questions to answer but I had to be careful.

I climbed on the bus feeling exhausted with the day. I was glad Field Day and my first dress day were behind me. The news of Cecelia's murder had hit me kind of hard for some reason. This meant that Arne really was a murderer. I had a murderer's letters. Maybe Detlef was right, maybe Arne was a traitor. I got home from school and found Tilly watching her favorite movie, Cinderella. My own room seemed like the best place to get a moment to relax.

Within minutes, Mom stormed into the room, "I know about what you did today. I know you changed into your gym clothes and didn't wear the dress." I was totally caught off guard. How did she know?

Racking my brain, I stopped suddenly. *It was Car-rie! That little brat...*

My face must have given me away, because Mom immediately defended her. "Don't blame Carrie for this, you made the choice yourself and you are grounded for two weeks. You will miss your friend's bonfire this weekend and you will wear a dress all next week."

"What is it with the dresses mom?" I asked and I knew my voice sounded snottier than it ever had before.

"Have a nice night in your room," Mom said sarcastically and she closed the door.

I was mostly relieved to be able to stay in my room for the night. My only visitors were Tigger, our cat, and Bernice, who dropped off my dinner. I guess Carrie knew better than to come near me tonight.

I spent some time secretly looking over the letters, wondering about the rest of the story. Then, decided to pull out my Bible and take a look inside. I knew God had been listening to me lately, but I couldn't seem to do the right thing. Why did I keep messing everything up? My bookmark was in John 15, because of last week's sermon. It was all about Jesus being like a grapevine and we are like the branches. I guess it meant that I would keep learning to obey God more if I stayed close to Him. I really wanted to stay close to Jesus.

Chapter 5

WHO WILL BE OUR NEXT PRESIDENT?

"Let your roots grow down into him, and let your lives be built on him. Then your faith will grow strong in the truth you were taught, and you will overflow with thankfulness."
Colossians 2:7 (NLT)

On November 8th 1988 citizens of the United States of America, over the age of eighteen, were invited to vote for a new president. The candidates were Michael Dukakis and George Bush. One of them would replace Ronald Reagan, who I liked so much.

I decided I liked him when I heard him give a speech in Germany. He said, "Mr. Gorbachev, tear down this wall!" I was not sure what the wall was all about, but I was sure it was a bad wall because tons of people cheered when the president said it should be torn down.

Our school had a mini election. We walked into a fake ballot box and cast our vote. Mrs. Hebner made it clear that we would not be able to do any real voting until we were 18; this was just for fun.

As we settled into our math lesson, I noticed a box by Mrs. Hebner's desk and as I tuned my ears in to the box, I thought I heard little feet moving around. I was pretty sure of what was in that box. Had anyone else noticed?

At recess, Michelle pulled a box of Jell-O mix out of her pocket and showed it to us. She was acting so sneaky that it seemed like she had drugs or something.

"I decided a long time ago, I would 'Just Say No,'" I tried to get a laugh. I don't think she got my joke.

"Why do you have that?" Christy asked.

"I eat it," she answered smugly. Then surprised us all when she generously added, "Do you want some?" We gathered around, not knowing what to expect. She opened one side of the bag and licked her finger. She dipped it deep into the dry strawberry

Jell-O mix and pulled out a red sugary finger. "Try some," she nudged the box against Kadie's hand as she licked her own finger happily.

"Well, strawberry is my favorite," Kadie shrugged. Christy, Kadie, and I all licked our finger and dunked again with no thought of the germs we were sharing.

"Wow, it's delicious," we all agreed. We spent the rest of recess trying not to be caught as we scarfed down Jell-o with our sticky red fingers.

As we walked back into the room with movie star lips, Mrs. Hebner was holding the lizard box. She asked us some questions to make sure we remembered all of the instructions. Then she opened the box and reached her hand through a rubber flap.

When she came to my group, she pulled a skinny little lizard out of the box and said it was mine. I was proud of how many strong looking vines had grown as she dropped him gently into our lush terrarium. He scurried around looking for a place to hide. I knew right away that his name was Snickers. Robby, Michelle, and Kadie each got a lizard too, but mine was the best.

In our books, we had learned that anoles turn different colors as they blend in with their surroundings. But to witness it was amazing. In a mere ten minutes, Snickers changed to green, then brown and back to green as he explored the terrarium.

The principal announced, at the end of the day, that Michael Dukakis won by a landslide in our school election. I was surprised, because my parents were voting for George Bush.

When I got home, and walked into the kitchen to look for a box of Jell-O, I was distracted by three cans sitting on the countertop. Those three cans meant one thing. Dinner tonight would be chop suey. One can of chicken, one can of slimy vegetables, and one can of worm noodles. I don't know when my mom discovered chop suey, but somehow, against my will, it was added to our regular meal schedule.

Whenever it was chop suey night, Bernice and I spent 20 minutes after dinner sitting at the table by ourselves slowly chewing small bites of worms. We had been banned from calling them worms since technically they weren't. But, in my head, they would always be worms. It was the only food Bernice and I tried to secretly dump in the garbage can last year, but we were caught and didn't get dessert for two weeks.

Later, as we sat down to eat dinner, Mom couldn't find Tilly.

"Tilly, dinnertime," She yelled. After a few minutes, little Tilly came downstairs wearing mom's lipstick with toilet paper sticking out of her pants. Reluctantly, I sat down to eat.

I quickly dished up a tiny scoop of worm sauce for me and Bernice, hoping no one would notice. Bernice gave me a grateful smile. Mom started some dinner conversation and it got interesting when she mentioned Arne.

"Mrs. Brown says the man who used to live here was always bringing them delicious pastries and she was shocked when she found out he was a Nazi and a m-u-r-d-e-r-e-r-." She raised her eyebrows at my dad who pretended to be surprised.

"What is a Nazi?" I asked, but I didn't get an answer, because all at once, we noticed an odd drip coming from the light fixture.

"It's raining in the house!" Tilly exclaimed as she began jumping up and down on her chair.

"That can't be good," said Mom as the dripping started moving faster and, to my delight, it trickled onto my plate.

Dad ran to the basement and the lights went off as the rest of us started clearing the table. Mom grabbed some candles and matches while Dad ran back upstairs yelling, "Maggie come help."

"The bathroom floor is completely flooded and the toilet is clogged," He reported, shaking his head in frustration. "Get some rags and disinfectant."

When I came back downstairs, Mom told us she had ordered pizza. She had also moved the dining room table and a bucket was sitting on the floor catching the remaining toilet water. We set up a candlelit picnic area in the living room.

The delicious pizza arrived. I hugged Tilly and said an extra prayer of thanks to God. Dad turned on the TV. On the news we saw a big map of the United States. The red states were the ones who seemed to have elected Mr. Bush. The blue states seemed to have more votes for Mr. Dukakis.

"I thought the president was Hammer-Ham Lincoln!" said Bernice.

"No, Abraham Lincoln was president more than 100 years ago" Mom tried to keep a straight face.

"Stop laughing," Bernice yelled at Carrie and I who couldn't stop no matter how hard we tried.

"It looks like our next president will be George Bush." Dad was pleased with the results.

I went to bed, long before all of the votes had been counted. It had been a great day!

Chapter 6

VERY INTERESTING

"And now, dear brothers and sisters, one final thing. Fix your thoughts on what is true, and honorable, and right, and pure, and lovely, and admirable. Think about things that are excellent and worthy of praise." Philippians 4:8 (NLT)

During the first weekend in December, I spent the night at Crystal's house. She was full of questions about my family. "Nothing new ever happens around here," she insisted. I tried to make my answers sound as interesting as possible. I loved my family, but I was pretty sure nothing about them was newsworthy. Not unless I mentioned the letters.

For most of the evening we walked around the neighborhood talking and eating ice cream. Crystal was tough, but she also cared about people. Even though I didn't always agree with her, she always had interesting things to say.

We walked through downtown. There was a small grocery store, the school, a gas station, a bar, an auto mechanic shop, and the ever-popular bowling alley. "Was there ever a bakery in Hillcrest?" I asked.

"Oh yeah, there was. You haven't heard the stories about the baker who murdered Davey's aunt?"

"What? I only knew a girl named Cecelia was murdered, and the baker went to prison. I don't know anything else. Tell me everything you know!"

"Well, my mom tells us a ghost story about Cecelia coming up outta the lake to find the one who killed her. My mom doesn't think it was the baker. She thinks it was another guy. But, the baker went to jail for murdering her." I could tell that Crystal thought it was exciting too.

"My family lives in the baker's old house." I admitted.

"No joke!" Crystal exclaimed. " Just wait til my mom hears where you live."

As we sat down for dinner, Crystal didn't waste

any time.

"Mom, Maggie lives in the house where the baking murderer lived."

"Yah don't say! Don't listen to Crystal, because believe you me, *da* baker never laid a finger on Cecelia." Crystal's mom corrected her. "That murder has been *eatin'* away at me for years." She stopped and peered at me intently.

"Cecelia worked for the baker. There was a rumor that her dad found out Cecelia was head over heels for her boss; who wasn't married, but he was *geeez*, 10 or 15 years older than her. Cecelia went away to Europe or *somethin'* for college and then I wanna say she was murdered within a month of coming home. The baker always seemed like he couldn't hurt a fly. Oh, I miss that bakery somethin' awful. But, the city tore the building down after he went to prison."

"Mom, you want him to be innocent so you can have your doughnuts back," accused Crystal. But, I wanted to believe Crystal's mom was right.

"So, if you don't think it was Arne who killed Cecelia, who do you think it was?"

"Geez, I shouldn't say...but I'll tell ya, da one I

think did it is an awful mixture of cheese and carbonation."

"I see." I nodded. "Wow, Crystal, you said that nothing ever happens in Hillcrest? This is an actual mystery."

The night went by slowly and I couldn't sleep. We watched a scary movie, but I tried my best to ignore it. The last thing I needed was another fear. Besides, I was thinking about Cecelia. I wondered who killed her. Was Crystal's mom right or did Arne have a mean streak? I had to know the truth!

When Mom came to pick me up the next morning, she saw Crystal for the first time. I hadn't thought much about Crystal's short spiky haircut since the first week I knew her, but my mom was in some state of shock. "Was that Crystal?" she asked.

"Yes," I answered, pretending not to know why she was using that tone.

"Whatever possessed her to get a haircut like that?"

"I don't know Mom. Can we talk about what a Nazi is instead? You said the man who owned our house was a Nazi."

Mom looked surprised but let me change the subject, "A Nazi is a person who followed a terrible ruler named, Adolf Hitler, who was in charge of Germany in the 1930's. Our country fought World War II to stop that ruler."

"If he was such a terrible ruler, why did people follow him?"

"That's a very good question. Sometimes people are scared to do what is right especially if they think they might get hurt for doing the right thing. I guess the man who used to own our house decided to stop following Hitler because he realized the leader of his country was hurting so many people."

That must be why his brother was so mad at him, I realized. *Arne was a good guy after all.*

Mom lowered her voice, "What's on your mind? I think it is more than Hitler.

"I thought adults were supposed to be smart." I blurted.

"Being wise is different than being smart. If fact, wisdom is more important. Adolf Hitler was quite smart but very cruel and foolish," she spoke carefully. "But no one is perfectly wise except God.

Not adults, not anyone."

I took a deep breath and realized again that God was the only one who knew the answers to so many of my questions.

Chapter 7

THE WALL IN THE MIDDLE OF THE CITY

"This means that God's holy people must endure persecution patiently, obeying his commands and maintaining their faith in Jesus." Revelation 14:12 (NLT)

Winter came and the air grew colder. The fishing lake we lived on began to freeze and snow covered everything like a cold blanket.

Mom planned one of her big movie nights. Of course, it involved picking numbers from a basket. They were seat numbers and there was a numbered map of each seat in the living room to go with it. The number we picked, decided our seat.   There was absolutely no trading allowed.

Mom let me pick the movie at the video store

and as soon as I saw the word "Germany" in the description, I grabbed, *Night Crossing*.

I got a seat by Tilly. She was sulking because we would not be watching Cinderella for the millionth time. Mom explained that the movie was about a family who made a hot air balloon and tried to get over The Berlin Wall. There were a few scenes we would be fast forwarding because there were scary parts.

"What would be scary about a balloon ride?" I asked.

Mom got out the globe and showed us East and West Germany. She explained that West Germany had freedom like the United States. But East Germany was controlled by the communist Soviet Union and the people did not have much freedom. It was even against the law to follow Jesus. When they first put up the wall, they used barbed wire and suddenly stopped everyone from crossing the border from East to West Germany. Only people who were high up in the government could move around freely.

Is *that the bad wall that president Reagan thinks should be torn down?* I wondered.

While we watched the movie, I was amazed at

the way the people all risked their life to be free. I couldn't imagine what it would be like to be so stuck in one place. The movie was also very helpful in my quest to understand the letters. The Stasi were a major part of the movie. They were the East German secret spy group who reported anyone who spoke badly about the government or broke the smallest law. When someone was reported, they got into big trouble and usually went to prison. Arne's brother was in the Stasi. That meant he was a bad dude.

I couldn't understand how a group of people would allow their rulers to make so many rules and a big wall that no one could cross. I decided, on Monday, I should go to the school library and see if I could learn more about this strange wall.

Chapter 8

GIRLY ENOUGH AFTER ALL

"I prayed to the Lord, and he answered me. He freed me from all my fears." Psalm 34:4 (NLT)

"Mags, wake up. Let's go sledding." It was Bernice and she was excited.

"Bernie, it's too early." I rolled over and hoped she would give up.

"Mags!" I heard her say behind me.

"Let's eat breakfast first." I answered and she pulled me into the kitchen to see what kind of cereal was in the cabinet.

I opened the cabinet, "Jackpot! Brown Sugar Pop-Tarts Bernice!"

We dropped them in the toaster and prepared for Pop-Tarts and milk. Soon, Carrie came out and cooked them the way she liked, burnt and sticky. She liked the way the brown sugar kind of turned to caramel.

I glanced down at the box and looked for the spot where it said, *Battle Creek* and showed it to my sisters. We felt nostalgic, but not sad because we had a long snowy hill waiting for us outside.

Dad was the sledding parent in our family. He rushed us out the door, suggesting he would use the old wooden sled to make the first run. I think he was afraid we'd fall into the lake at the end of the hill.

We watched as he moved quickly down the hill. He stopped before he reached the three foot drop that went into the lake. Hazy Lake was frozen, but we agreed, it wasn't frozen enough.

Dad yelled, "Come on down," as he started his walk up the hill. All three of us jumped in the sled with Carrie in front. We made it down the hill in record time. As we walked up the hill, we saw our mom watching with a smile. Tilly and Annika tapped on the window from inside. I knew they were begging mom to bring them outside. Mom wasn't much of an outdoors lady.

As we went back into the house to warm up our fingers and toes, I knew Mom was in a good mood. She had pulled out her favorite cookbook and was mixing delicious smelling ingredients on the stove. We rated everything she made out of this cookbook. Mom refused to skip a single recipe. Even when she came to one called Carrot Quiche, she made it. She didn't care that it took two hours to make and we all knew it would get a "Terrible" rating. Thankfully, the Parmesan Chicken earned a, "Very good."

On Monday, I got my chance to go to the library and grab some books about East Germany and the Berlin Wall. When I jumped on the bus, I opened the first book. It was a bit confusing because it kept mentioning something called the Cold War and I didn't know anything about the Cold War. It seemed like after Adolf Hitler and Germany lost World War II, Germany was split in half, West Germany and East Germany.

The United States, Great Britain, and France got half of Germany to help run it the way they thought it should be run. The Soviet Union got a smaller half of Germany to help run it the way they wanted. The problem was, many people -like *millions* of people- left the Eastern part of Germany and moved to West Germany. The Soviet Union must have gotten jealous, because they built the wall in 1961 and said they would shoot anyone who tried to cross the wall back over into West Germany. Note to dictators: if you have to put up a wall to keep people in, your country has major problems.

On top of being trapped, the people who lived in East Germany were forced to follow a ton of rules. They weren't allowed to make their own choices about what they watched on TV, what religion they followed, or which job they had.

The pictures of the Berlin Wall were interesting, because one side of the wall, the West Side, was covered in painted pictures and messages about peace and freedom. The East Side was completely blank. More than 150 people had been killed trying to escape over the wall. People had died trying to dig tunnels under the wall or hide in secret places in cars when they passed through the gate.

When I got home I had a good talk with my mom about East Germany. She helped me understand some of the complicated parts. She said that many Christians in East Germany met secretly to study the Bible and follow Jesus. She said the government didn't want the people to believe in God, because then they would be able to be more brave and love more, which would make the government have less power. We prayed for people in East Germany who knew Jesus and needed God's help to be brave. We prayed for people in East Germany who had never heard the truth about Jesus. We prayed with President Reagan that the wall would come down.

I realized that Mom didn't seem quite so worried about me. Even though I had a lizard for a pet (which grossed her out), I didn't like wearing dresses (which she thought was scary), and my palms were covered in calluses (which freaked her out). I guess she had decided I was girly enough, after all.

Chapter 9

CHRISTMAS BREAK

But the angel said to them, "Do not be afraid. I bring you good news of great joy. It is for all the people. Today in the town of David a Savior has been born to you. He is Christ the Lord…" Luke 2:10-11 (NIV)

On the last day of school, before Christmas break, we reluctantly took apart our classroom terrariums. As I expected, Mom said there was no way she would allow a lizard to live in our house. Knowing Mom's fear of all non-cat animals, I couldn't blame her. So, I said goodbye to Snickers and, as planned, he went home with Crystal.

At Christmas time, Mom loved to go and pick out a tree taller than our ceiling and then bring it home and ask my dad to try to figure out how to make it fit. It was always a bit lopsided and would randomly fall over while we were eating dinner, or in the middle of the night. Mom blamed the cat, but we knew better.

Dad liked several of the old Christmas movies. He usually forced us to sit down to watch the old, black and white version of A Christmas Carol. Somehow, he hoped it would make us more grateful and maybe it did.

My sisters and I all slept in my room on Christmas Eve. When we woke up, we ran and banged on Mom and Dad's door.

"It's six o'clock in the morning. Give us one more hour," they begged.

We went back to the bedroom. Eventually, we heard Dad come out to make coffee. We didn't dare take a peek down the hallway to the living room where the tree sat. The torturous waiting was half the fun.

Finally, after twenty minutes or so, everyone was ready and we helped Annika walk slowly down the hall to the tree. She had no idea what was going on, but since we were all excited, she was too. Dad and Mom had turned on the tree lights and we could see all of the gifts.

The first thing we did was sit down to listen while Dad read the Christmas story from the beginning of the book of Luke. My favorite part of the story was when the angels appeared. I could just imagine the sky filled with angels celebrating the King of all of the Kings coming to this earth, as a baby.

Our first gifts were clothes. Then we each opened our toy gifts. Bernice's first gift was very predictable. Two years ago, she had started a porcelain doll collection and every birthday and Christmas she would get a new doll. She liked them, but they just sat on the shelf in her room. However, the benefit of liking porcelain dolls was that it automatically made you girly enough. No one forced a porcelain doll collector to wear dresses.

Carrie got a Barbie, and I got a set of Little People characters with vehicles. I was not ashamed of the fact that the package said it was for ages two to six.

Tilly opened some Little Peoples too and a Peter Pan movie. We were all so glad she'd have something, other than Cinderella, to watch.

Then we each opened some books. I got a Nancy Drew Mystery to add to my collection. Inside of my book was a five-dollar gift certificate to Hill's Cheese Soda Shop. The family all laughed because they loved to tease me for being the only one willing to drink Cheese Soda. Little did they know I'd been looking for a chance to scope out the cheese soda shop and see if I could find any clues to the devious workings of Mr. Hill, the potential murderer.

Soon, our attention was on the biggest boxes. They looked like boot boxes, but we already had boots.

Dad and Mom looked excited and told us to open them at the same time.

"Oh my goodness," Carrie shrieked. As we opened the paper and realized, in our hands we each had a pair of brand new ice skates. Bernice squealed with glee.

Mom said, "Dad already has a pair of old skates and we think the ice will be solid enough for you to skate by the time we get back from Michigan." We could hardly wait.

The day after Christmas we traveled the seven hours south around Lake Michigan, through Chicago and into Michigan to get together with our Pierce and Pullman family. We all forgot the time change and ended up arriving at my grandma's house an hour early.

Our Grandma Bea was the classic grandma in many ways. She slept with curlers in her hair, baked tons of cookies, and wore the cutest aprons. When Grandma Bea watched the news, she yelled at the TV for almost the whole hour. I learned a lot about politics from listening. When it came to the world news, Grandma did not mess around.

Our cousin Jenny, from California, was visiting too. She was three years older than me and so cool. She played tennis and talked about music groups as if she knew them.

Whenever Jenny visited, my grandma gave her extra attention. Sometimes, I got a little jealous.

That evening, Sara, Carrie, and I talked for hours. My mind kept going back to that crazy wall in Berlin.

"Wake up!" I heard Carrie and Sara saying and I realized I was daydreaming.

"What were you thinking so deeply about?" Sara asked.

"It's kind of weird. I answered, but I was thinking about how great it is to be able to visit Michigan without any problem. In East and West Germany the people can't even visit their family on the other side of the wall." Sara and Carrie agreed it would stink to live in a place where you would be killed for trying to visit your family.

"Okay, enough talking, let's play," Carrie declared.

We decided to play hide and seek. I hid in the cellar. While I was hiding, I heard Grandma talking to Jenny. "Jenny, will you go down to the cellar and grab me two cans of peaches?"

"Sure Grandma" said Jenny obediently. All at once, I got a sneaky idea.

"I found Mags," Carrie yelled as I ran out of the cellar and to the back corner of the basement, behind the couch.

"What in the world are you doing?" Carrie asked as she and Sara followed me to the corner.

"I'm hiding all of the peaches from grandma and Jenny," I whispered, shoving the cans of peaches under the couch while catching my breath. Out of the corner of my eye I saw an unsuspecting Jenny traveling into the cellar. I was pretty sure she was not going to find any peaches, but I watched to see what would happen and while I watched, I explained. We watched as Jenny came out of the cellar with a confused look and headed straight up the stairs.

I whispered, "Come on!" and ran for the cellar where I knew we'd be able to hear what Jenny said.

"Grandma, there aren't any peaches left," Jenny informed her.

"Oh, you must not have looked closely, because I know we have several cans on the second shelf in the back." she explained.

"Okay, Grandma, I'll look one more time," Jenny said and we ran as fast as we could out of the cellar trying to act nonchalant as she came down the stairs to the basement.

"Jenny, what are you doing?" Sara asked innocently. Jenny mumbled something about peaches and walked back into the cellar.

After a few minutes, Jenny went upstairs again and we ran back into the cellar. We knew we were in trouble when we heard Grandma Bea say, "I'm gonna go take a look."

My grandma was a very organized lady, and if she said there were peaches in the cellar then you had better believe there were peaches in the cellar.

We each grabbed two cans of peaches and dropped them back on the second shelf, in time to hear grandma coming down the stairs.

"We're trapped!" We frantically slipped in the crawl space under the stairs.

Grandma Bea opened the door while Jenny explained to her, "I looked through the whole cellar, Grandma."

I stifled a giggle imagining what might happen next.

"I see several cans right here on the second shelf," Grandma said in a perplexed voice.

"That's impossible!"

After Jenny and Grandma went back upstairs, we couldn't help but follow and that was our first mistake. One glance and Grandma knew we were up to no good.

"Did you ladies have anything to do with my missing peaches?" she asked. We laughed a guilty laugh and were relieved to see Jenny and Grandma smile. Grandma also looked very surprised. I'm not sure if she was amazed to learn we would do something so sneaky or if she was amazed at our stealth skills. Mostly, I think she was relieved to find out that Jenny was not going crazy.

"Sorry Jenny." I explained how I was in the cellar and couldn't resist. She didn't seem mad at all.

We had a wonderful time with the whole Pullman family and the Pierce family too.

Mom was especially sad when it was time to leave Michigan. We were sad too, but we knew that going back to Wisconsin meant it was time to go skating.

When we arrived home and walked in the door, the house was freezing. We noticed right away that the bathroom sink wouldn't turn on and my mom and dad realized the furnace must have stopped while we weren't home.

Mom gave Dad the 'why did you move us here?' look and Dad said, "I'd better go check the basement."

A few seconds later we heard Dad yell. "Susie, come take a look." Mom rushed downstairs and my sisters and I all gathered at the top of the staircase to listen. The basement was covered in water.

It ended up that the pilot light had gone out and the pipes were frozen. For the next day, everyone pitched in to clean up water while dad repaired the pipes. For all of Sunday dad was exhausted, but by Monday when he got home from work, we couldn't wait another second. We just had to go skating!

We bundled up, but instead of boots, we put on skates. We went out, hopped on our sleds and this time we didn't stop when we got to the drop-off that went into the lake. Instead, we let out a scream of pain as we flew through the air and hit the ice at full speed.

Finally, my dad slid down the hill. "Why didn't you wait for me," he asked.

"Why didn't you warn us that we should duct tape pillows to our bums?" Carrie rubbed her bruises looking for sympathy.

Dad came out on the ice and started to show off his skills.

"Teach us?" we begged. He took Bernice's hand and slowly helped her to her feet. Then he reached for Carrie with the other hand. He instructed Carrie to hold my hand and we wobbled forward.

"Now, slowly slide one foot forward. Keep

your foot straight. Then slide the other foot slowly forward. Left, right, left. If you feel yourself falling, fall forward and use your hands and knees to break the fall," he instructed. After fifteen minutes of wobbling, we were skating on our own. We weren't going to be trying out for the Olympics any time soon, but we could get around.

During the next few days, our quiet lake turned into a thriving community of fisher-people. We had never seen anything like it. There must have been fifteen trucks on our little lake and huts with people inside. There were dozens of buckets with fish that had been pulled up from their wet winter homes and would soon be on dinner plates. It was all so new and exciting.

There were a few fisher-people who rested just yards from our property. We tried to talk with them a little, but it was too cold and too hard to communicate through all of the layers of clothing we were wearing.

One day Bernice and I went for a skate. It was fun to skate around the village of ice shanties on the lake. We could cut and weave in and out of each one. As we approached one of the huts I saw a pair of familiar brown eyes. "Davey," I exclaimed before I was even sure it was him. He put down his pole and rubbed his hands together obviously trying to keep warm.

"So, you're a professional ice skater!" he teased.

"Ha-ha!" I laughed.

I asked if he had caught anything. "I'm having walleye for dinner tonight!" he pointed to the bucket. Just then his dad stepped out of the hut and I was proud of my maturity when I reached out my gloved hand and said, "Hello, Mr. Philips. I'm Maggie."

"Well hello young lady!" Davey's dad said with a smile.

"Maggie, I need to go potty!" Bernice pulled on my coat.

"Well I'd better get going" I turned toward Bernice and skated away.

That night we added a ramp to our sledding hill to make the trip down to the lake less painful. Our backyard was now the perfect winter playground and I temporarily forgot my mystery. Winter break had been a huge success!

Chapter 10

ONE BAD DECISION RUINS THE FUN

Proverbs 13:1 "A wise child accepts a parent's discipline; a mocker refuses to listen to correction." (NLT)

Mrs. Stinson, the librarian, was so excited to have a student who wanted to study history. "What did you learn?" she asked as I turned in the books on my first day back to school.

"Well, I learned the Berlin Wall was built in 1961 because East Germany was afraid all of their people were going to move to the West. I read that the people in the East are pretty much trapped and they don't have many rights. It's really sad."

"You learned quite a bit. Would you like to learn about other groups of people who are going through hard times?" I nodded because she looked so excited.

"Are there worse things than this happening in the world?"

"You can decide which you think is worse" she handed me a newspaper article and magazine with pictures of hundreds of thin, dark skinned boys. I noticed the dates for the articles were from 1988. As I read, I learned that thousands of villages, in Sudan, were attacked and the young boys from the cities were sent away because of the violence. They had to leave their country fast. The boys walked from Sudan all the way to Ethiopia looking for help, without their parents or other adults. The oldest ones (who were only twelve years old) had to be in charge. Some of them were still walking to a little camp where they could get just enough food to survive.

In the pictures, the boys looked so tired, but their eyes were very wide open and they just looked like they were waiting with hope. My eyes filled with tears as I realized these were real people who were my age and so brave.

"Wow, this is worse than what is happening in Germany," I concluded. "How could anyone do this to children?"

"I don't understand it either," Mrs. Stinson said. "But, I think it is important to know about what they have been through. Remembering what they are going through helps us to make better choices."

But, what could I do for any of those people? I left the library feeling helpless.

After lunch, was the annual spelling bee. I already knew, from my last school, that I stunk at spelling bees. During the one in Battle Creek I misspelled my first word. My friend and I had so much time after we missed our word that we decided to do each other's hair. She ended up tying my hair into such an enormous knotty mess that my mom had to cut my hair when I got home.

The spelling bee in Hillcrest was much more organized. We were all in the lunchroom instead of being jammed into one classroom. As I stood in line waiting, I tried to predict my word and rehearse what I would say. If the teacher said, "spell peanut," then my plan was to say, "peanut, P-E-A-N-U-T, peanut."

Davey, Kadie, and my sister Carrie spelled their first round word correctly. When it was my turn, the teacher said, "The word is pumpkin." I looked around the room and saw hundreds of curious eyes on me. They seemed to know that I was about to fail. I panicked and began to spell the word without repeating it. "p-u-m," *Oh no, I forgot*! "pumpkin, p-u-m-k-i-n, pumpkin." I finished with a feeling of victory, which only lasted a moment.

I heard the teacher say, "Incorrect" and she gave my word to the next person. "Pumpkin." I sat down at the lunch table where the three other kids who couldn't spell were sitting. I wondered if Davey was disappointed with my spelling skills. Maybe he was eyeing my sister for the first time and thinking, "Why haven't I ever noticed Maggie's sister with the cute brown curls before?" After all, how embarrassing, my little sister was a better speller than me. I saw Kadie give me a reassuring look and decided to silently root for her.

Kadie made it to round three. Carrie got third place. Davey won second place. Christy, the girl with the beautiful curly hair, who was good at everything, was the winner.

On the way to art class, after the spelling bee, I heard Davey's best friend Kevin singing something funny behind me. It sounded like he was singing a song with my name in it. I turned and gave him a funny look. He smiled with a suspicious smile and I wondered what was happening.

On the way back from art, I heard it again. This time the words were a little clearer. "Davey likes Maggie, he told me on the bus." There was more to the song, but the rest didn't matter. I looked for Davey, to see if he heard and he was looking back at me. He didn't seem embarrassed at all. I looked away in surprise. My entire body froze in fear. I gasped a little, realizing that for a minute, I had forgotten to breathe.

I went on with the day, trying to act normal. On the bus ride home, Carrie was in an extra good mood after winning the third place spelling bee ribbon. She was excited about the Davey thing too. She told me I should wait and see what happened, but try not to be afraid to talk to him, because he must like me too.

That night Mom finally took me to Hill's Cheese Soda Shop to spend my five dollars and do some secret detective work. All of my sisters came. My mom said it was just like an old-fashioned soda shop. There was even a cheese sundae and a cheese float on the menu. Mom chased Tilly and Annika around so I could browse. Carrie and Bernice couldn't seem to stop laughing about all of the funny cheese products so Mom sent them back out to sit in the car. I probably would have been laughing too if I had not been so focused on my secret mission.

A sales girl came and asked me how she could help. I took the opportunity to ask, "Do you get to see Mr. Hill very much?"

"Yea," she replied, "I see him and his wife pretty much every time I work. He's here now, if you would like his autograph. He just loves to give autogra..."

"That's okay," I interrupted. "I was just wondering if you like working for him."

"Mag's can you hurry it up?" said Mom with emphasis on hurry, "We didn't come here so you could ask questions about the owner. Do you see anything you would like to *BUY*?"

I found a variety bag of cheese flavored jellybeans and went to the counter where the cashier met me and let me know Mr. Hill would be out to sign something for me in just a moment. I thanked her and searched my coat pocket for a scrap of paper. Mom flashed me a puzzled look and I motioned that I wasn't sure what was going on as Mr. Hill came over, pen in hand, and signed my jellybeans.

He was a short man of around fifty years old wearing a designer Cheese Soda sweat suit and a big wide smile. His hair reminded me of something on the head of a Ken doll and I couldn't tell if it was real. He smiled and nodded his super shiny brown head of hair. He looked so pleased that I wanted his autograph and suddenly I didn't want to disappoint him. Could this man be a murderer, I wondered? I tried to look deep into his eyes for the answer as I thanked him for his time.

There was only one way to find out the truth. Still, I was pretty sure if I asked him, "Did you kill Cecelia Walsh?" my mom would have me committed to one of those homes for defiant adolescents. So, I kept my mouth shut and focused on moving forward.

Soon, it was the weekend. Carrie, Bernice, and I all had friends coming to spend the night. We were hoping to take them on the ice, but Mom said it wasn't safe anymore.

I invited Lena. As soon as she arrived, we went for a walk down the street. It was March and there wasn't much to see in our quiet neighborhood with houses on one side of the street and forest on the other.

As we were talking, Lena pulled out a bottle of Tylenol.

"Why do you have medicine in your coat pocket?" I asked.

"I just like them," she answered matter-of-factly.

"I thought you're only supposed to take them when you're sick," I questioned naively. She opened the bottle and pulled out four pills. I watched in horror as she popped them into her mouth and jerked her head back to show me she had swallowed them all. I didn't even try to hide how worried I was. For all I knew a person would die from taking four Tylenol at once.

"Lena, please don't take anymore. Give me the bottle," I insisted.

"Don't have a cow. I do this all the time."

"But why do you take medicine if you're not sick?" She knew I didn't understand, but she didn't want to give me an answer.

We decided to go back to the house to look for a movie to watch. As I read off the names of our movies,

Annika came running into the room wearing a straw hat and a diaper. Lena laughed for the first time all evening because Annika put on a big show.

Lena wasn't interested in watching any of our movies. So, we went downstairs to play *Yahtzee*. I offered her some cheese-flavored jellybeans. It was the only candy in the house. The scorecards were yellowed from age, but at the top of the scorecard I noticed two names, Arne and Cecelia. I grabbed the page and folded it into my pocket. The handwriting looked exactly like the handwriting from Cecelia's letters.

The game was fun. We both laughed at how horrible the jellybeans tasted, as we ate the whole bag. The Swiss cheese bean was the worst.

We stayed up late talking and painting our fingernails with crazy designs. She told me more about her mom's frustrating boyfriends, like the one who ate all of their food but refused to get a job. The week before, the guy had eaten a whole box of her favorite cereal by the time Lena got home from school. I didn't know what to say. Her life was so different from mine. We thought of funny jokes we could play on him like putting hot sauce in the cereal or replacing his favorite movies with cartoons.

In the morning, after breakfast, Mom asked if I would take Bernice and her friend Brooke for a walk. As we walked, I kept looking down the hill between the houses at the lake. It looked fairly frozen. There weren't any more cars on the ice, but it looked like it was still solid. "Bernice, let's go out on the ice. We won't go out far," I suggested.

"Mom told us we can't anymore," came the wise words from her six-year-old mouth.

"Please Bernie," I pleaded. "Lena and Brooke need a chance to get out on the ice," I pressured her. Lena perked up, ready for some adventure. I was sure she couldn't believe I wanted to disobey. We walked between the houses down the street to the lake's edge. Bernice and Brooke followed reluctantly.

On the edge, we could see a lot of ice with an inch or so of water on top and I considered changing my mind. But I looked out a few yards and saw solid looking ice.

"We need to hold hands and take a big step," I instructed as if I knew what I was doing. I grabbed Lena and Bernice's hands. Bernice grabbed Brooke's hand and we took our first big step. We let out a little squeal when we felt our shoes getting wet, but the ice held our weight. Slowly, we ventured out a few more feet onto the lake. It didn't seem too bad. We walked further and heard a deep down cracking sound. Bernice and Brooke began crying loudly. I looked up to see how far from home we were. We were four houses from home.

"I just want to walk on the ice to our house," I said selfishly.

I wanted to say, "don't worry, the ice is our friend. We've played on the ice all winter."I wanted to say, "Bernice, where is your loyalty? You know we can trust this ice."

Suddenly, the cracking got worse. I looked out to where the ice shanties had been all winter, but there were no fisher-people today. All at once, I realized I'd made a terrible mistake. We continued to creep along slowly, looking for the places where the ice looked strongest. We were trying to work our way back to the shore, but there were places where the ice looked very weak. By now, Bernice and Brooke were in a complete state of panic, and Lena might have been more scared than she'd ever been, but I didn't have the option of panicking because I knew this was entirely my fault.

"My feet are frozen," whimpered Brooke.

All of a sudden, we heard a welcomed voice. "Its Mom," Bernice and I said at the same time. I didn't even care how much trouble I was going to be in. I was so relieved,

She motioned for us to come to her slowly. She was freaking out.

"Be careful!" Mom cried desperately.

When we were only about 10 feet from shore, Bernice's little right foot poked a slushy hole in the ice, her right leg sunk all the way to her knee before Lena, and I both grabbed her. She let out a shrill scream as we pulled her toward us. We all clumped together because we didn't want to risk another move.

"Keep walking to me. Slowly," Mom tried to keep us focused.

"Let's go!" I said, holding their hands tightly continuing toward shore one prayerful step at a time. As Brooke, then Bernice, then Lena and I fi8nally took our first step onto land we slumped to the ground where my mom wrapped a blanket around us and we took our frozen feet into the house.

I hugged each of the girls apologetically.

"I'm sorry." I kept saying, "I know Mom, I'm sorry." Mom tried to convince me of the dangers of thin ice, and then sent me to my room and called Brooke and Lena's parents. Within an hour she had taken them both home and I could hear her in the living room talking on the phone to my dad. It was the same tone I'd heard many times before. It was the "what is happening to our little girl" tone. I was grounded for a month. I deserved worse.

Within an hour, my dad knocked on the door of my bedroom. "Maggie, what got into you?" he started. "We can usually trust you, especially with your sisters."

I didn't know how to answer any of their questions. I was as surprised as everyone else. The thought of going to school was so embarrassing. I didn't want to face Lena and I was sure the whole kindergarten class would be pointing at me, saying "there's the girl who almost killed our friends."

I remembered to talk to God about this problem and I think He talked back because I suddenly realized I should be thankful that no one got hurt. He was protecting us. I was foolish, but He showed me mercy. Somehow I knew He had forgiven me. He still loved me.

Chapter 11

THAT IS SERIOUS

"Do everything without complaining and arguing, so that no one can criticize you. Live clean, innocent lives as children of God, shining like bright lights in a world full of crooked and perverse people." Philippians 2:14-15 (NIV)

The end of March and beginning of April crept by. It seemed like no matter how hard I tried to fight it, I was grumpy. I had extra chores and spent a lot of time playing with Annika and Tilly. Tilly and I built a Little People's village like the world had never seen before. There was a skyway they could use to travel across town and even a Pizza Hut.

My mood got even worse when I came home from school one day and saw that Annika had knocked it all over. I told her, "That's a no-no." She must have liked how that sounded because for a week, she walked around the house with a mean look on her face, pointing her finger and saying, "Datz a no-no!"

Before we left for the grocery store one day, I remembered I needed some books about The Great Depression. I knew I could get the books from the school library, but if I went to the Columbus library I could finally see the newspaper articles about Cecelia and Arne.

Mom agreed to let me stay at the library alone while she shopped. I grabbed some dimes from the change jar and wondered if I'd find anything good to copy. Quickly, I found three books about The Great Depression. When I asked if they had the Columbus newspaper for all of 1961, the librarian handed me a roll of microfiche and showed me how to insert it into the magnifying window so that I could read the old newspaper articles.

On June 16th, 1961, I saw an article about the trial of Arne Werfel. I read the pages that followed and learned it was a fast trial. There was no body found, but a canoe was found with Cecelia's jacket, a book, and two strands of her hair. In the same canoe, there was a thermos with Arne's handprints, a strand of his hair, and two of his pastries. Arne said he was innocent but he was sentenced to life in prison. I figured it might be time to tell my mom that the man we bought our house from, who was now in prison, might actually be innocent.

Then I spotted it. He looked just the way I had imagined him; light hair, kind eyes, thick eyebrows and a strong looking jaw. This was Arne.

No! Under the picture, in big bold letters, it said, MURDERER!!! Well actually it said, "First degree murderer, Arne Werfel. This was what everyone thought. How could they have been so wrong?

As I placed my new research into my backpack, I felt like the clues were beginning to line up. I wondered if one of the smart librarians might be able to understand the weird number in the last letter from Cecelia.

Immediately, the first librarian I asked called it an ISBN number. She led me to a shelf and pulled out a book called, *Billiards at Half-past Nine*. She said it was a German Novel, written by Heinrich Boll and it would be hard for me to read.

"I just need to see one page," I said reaching for the book. On page 204, four words were underlined in pencil, "*He ordered me to*."

"That's it! You may have just helped a man get

out of prison." With a burst of hope, I hugged the startled librarian and checked out my first German novel.

Safely back in the van, I ran my fingers over the penciled line that could only have been written by Cecelia herself. I felt connected to her in a way I couldn't describe. These were the words Cecelia wanted Arne to read. Who was "he"? Was "he" Mr. Hill? What did "he" order Cecelia to do? I had to find the truth. I assumed, Cecelia would have wanted me to help.

The only other exciting thing that happened all month was when the pastor preached another sermon I understood. It was about true worship. We looked at Psalm 26:10 where God says, "Be still, and know that I am God; I will be exalted among the nations, I will be exalted in the earth." I sat and tried to remember some of the amazing things I knew about God and think about those things.

I knew He made plants wonderful, with seeds so there is always a way to grow a new one. Oranges grow from flowers and they don't turn orange until they are ripe. Then you open the skin and find perfectly protected juice inside with bite size pieces so you don't even need a knife. Oranges amazed me and they were obviously created by God.

Also, He gave us the Bible that teaches us about how He loves all the people He created. Even though we sin so much He made a way to take our punishment. I closed my eyes and tried to be still for a couple of minutes. I think I was truly worshipping God. It was a secret moment between Him and me and I think He was pleased.

One morning in mid-April, my class arrived to find a substitute teacher sitting at Mrs. Hebner's desk. At first we were excited, but the teacher explained that Mrs. Hebner's Dad passed away suddenly and she would be gone for a week. The whole class felt awful and we made her cards, but it was so hard to decide what to write. Finally, I wrote "I'm so sorry about what happened. You are a super teacher," on the card.

During lunch, Crystal told me she was so sorry, but she lost my little lizard. She had taken the lizards outside for some fresh air. Little Snickers started to get away so she grabbed him by his tail but it fell off and he got away. I couldn't be mad at her.

"Don't worry," I told her. "If Snickers had come to my house he would have been attacked by a screaming woman with a broom.

"Still, I'm pretty sure he's…" and Crystal made a cutthroat motion across her neck.

"Let's just hope he made it all the way down to Arkansas and found a quiet tree all to himself."

After all the talk about death, I finally asked my mom about how dangerous taking four Tylenol at once could be. I knew I had practically gotten Lena killed, but that didn't mean I should let her hurt herself. My mom said taking all of that Tylenol was really dangerous and even if nothing terrible happened all at once, she said it would hurt a person's liver and other organs. I decided to try talking to Lena again about the Tylenol. This time, I'd be more prepared.

I had noticed lately that trying on words was a lot like trying on clothes. The only difference was, when it comes to words we don't need to pay to use them. Anyone, no matter how much money they have, can choose their own words. Well, sort of…

In my house, there were a few words that were forbidden. If you asked my mom, she would tell you these words were all of the typical curse words, plus some others like, butt-head. If you asked my dad, he told you that the prohibited words are the typical ones, plus "*ain't*." He was very strict about grammar.

But, the very worst thing you could do with your words in my house was to take the Lord's name in vain. Until yesterday I hadn't considered the reason why it was so important. I just knew that I'd better not yell His name when I got a sliver or saw a cat that had been hit by a car.

Then Kadie got me thinking when she asked, "What does it mean to take God's name in vain?"

I had to think about it for a while. Then I told her, "I think it's about using God's name carefully and giving Him respect because He is God and He deserves all of our respect." I think she understood what I meant.

On my way back from choir I stopped in the bathroom and Lena was there. It was my first chance to talk to her alone since what happened on the lake. I was afraid to bring it up. "I'm sorry I took you out on the lake that day." I started.

"It's okay," she said genuinely.

"I know I was bugging you about the Tylenol and then I almost made you drown."

"Well, I know it's stupid to take all of that Tylenol. Sometimes, when it's late, and my mom is working and I'm so bored, I just want to swallow a whole bottle."

"Please don't ever do that." I gave her a hug and wondered if I should tell someone.

"Don't tell anyone, okay? I won't really do it," she waited for my answer.

"Okay," I agreed reluctantly.

As I tried to get to sleep, I felt uneasy about the whole day. I wondered if I should tell someone about the Tylenol Lena took. I was afraid if I did, Lena would hate me.

And then there was the mystery of Arne and Cecelia. I was beginning to think the mystery would never be solved. I needed more information.

Chapter 12

BEAUTY STRESS

"Don't be concerned about the outward beauty of fancy hairstyles, expensive jewelry, or beautiful clothes. You should clothe yourselves instead with the beauty that comes from within, the unfading beauty of a gentle and quiet spirit, which is so precious to God." 1 Peter 3:3-4 (NIV)

It was my birthday. I had asked for stirrup pants and a mood ring. As I climbed out of bed and made my way into the bathroom, I glimpsed in the mirror. There I saw a single, large, red, crusty bump. As I continued to examine my pimple in the mirror, I pulled out my toothbrush to brush my teeth, but instead of using it on my teeth I decided to brush this big red pimple.

Brushing it didn't seem to help. In fact, it was

starting to ooze. Someone knocked on the bathroom door and when I said, "Come in," Dad appeared.

He noticed immediately what I was doing and asked with an agitated laugh, "What in the world are you doing to your face?"

"Look Dad," I showed him the bump and fully expected he would jump back in horror when he saw it.

"That is hardly even noticeable," he said instead. "Just leave it alone and it will go away."

Was my dad really qualified to give medical advice? I walked down the hall in what he would call a huffy way. *I bet no one will even remember it's my birthday*, I thought.

"Happy birthday!" Carrie said just then and everyone else chimed in.

School was completely normal until recess. Kadie gave me the best gift I had ever received: a friendship necklace with a heart that was broken in half. She wore the other necklace and I felt so special.

To top it off, on the way out the door at the end of the day, Davey handed me a card. I said thank you and tried to hide my excitement until I got on the bus. Then, I looked at the envelope where "MAGGIE" was written in tidy letters. I pulled out the card. On the front was a picture of a cute little kitten. It read, "I hope your birthday is ..." I opened the card to find the words "purrrrrfec..." My eyes stopped short of reading the message because they caught the words at the bottom. The words were "Love, David"

What did it mean? Did it mean love, like "I love you?" No way! Maybe, "Love" like... "the word 'From' seemed boring so I picked the word 'Love.'"

And why did he sign his name David? Did he want me to call him David? I didn't know anyone who called him David.

Carrie hopped on the bus and I urgently motioned for her to sit with me. She sat down and I handed her the card to read for herself. She was even more shocked then me. "What do I say tomorrow?" I asked, looking for the perfect response.

As I lay in bed that night trying to get to sleep, I reflected on the day. It seemed like a wonderful dream. Still, there was something that was bothering me, but I couldn't remember what it was. Then, I remembered Lena. I only had two weeks til summer vacation. I had to figure out what to do about Lena and the pills. I couldn't ignore the problem. I needed a plan.

Then, there was Arne. I was still convinced he was an innocent man sitting in prison somewhere, while the real murderer walked free. Could it be Mr. Hill, or someone else? Then I realized I was worrying and decided to talk to God about it all. After all, He was the only One who knew what was best for Lena or Arne and He might be the only One who knew the truth.

Dear God,

You know that I worry so much. Sometimes it's hard to know what to do with my worries. I like to just push all of the worries away and do nothing but ignore them. Sometimes the worries get smaller when I do. But, I'm learning that you can take care of the worries when I give them to you. You will help me know what to do. Please help me know what to do and help Lena. Thank you for listening to me and for helping.

The next day, I made my weekly trip to the school library after lunch. I was glad to see that there were no other students and I decided it was time. As I made the decision I felt a mixture of relief and guilt, but I decided to stop thinking so much and start talking.

"Mrs. Stinson..."

"Oh Maggie, did you read that book about Cambodia?"

"Not yet, but I want to talk to you about something else."

"Okay, what is it?"

"Well, what would you do, if you had a friend who was taking a lot of pills and hurting herself?" I spit the words out all at once.

"That's a tough one. It would depend on whether this person was a child or an adult."

"This person is a kid."

"I would want to make sure that she got some help, because if this child is hurting herself, she probably needs some help very soon."

These were the words I was afraid I would hear. I had no choice, but to spill the beans, promise or no promise. "Mrs. Stinson, do you know Lena Rivers?"

"Yes I do. Is she the friend you are talking about?"

"Yes, she's been taking a lot of Tylenol, but I promised her I wouldn't tell anyone."

Mrs. Stinson seemed to understand what I meant. She asked me a few more questions and then assured me that she would take it from here. Mrs. Stinson said I should keep quiet about it now because she would make sure that Lena got help.

Later that day, Mrs. Stinson stepped into the classroom and asked for Lena to come help her sort books. When Lena returned to class she looked like she had been crying, but she didn't look sad, she looked relieved.

Two days passed and I had taken care of the situation with Lena, but I hadn't said a word to Davey, I mean David.

The perfect opportunity finally arrived when I climbed onto the bus for our field trip. David was sitting in a seat all by himself. I decided to be gutsy and sit down next to him. On the way, we drove by his family's farm and he pointed it out to me proudly.

He told me they had 200 cows and 150 acres of

land they cared for and it sounded like a lot of hard work. My life at home was filled with sisters and his was filled with cows.

"Thank you so much for the card. I'm serious! It made my day." I said, relieved that I'd finally thanked him.

"Well, I wanted you to know that I remembered your birthday," he explained in a tone that made my heart want to burst.

I smiled and I knew it was a nervous and excited smile. I wanted to ask him about the "love" part, but I knew I never would. I looked at him, and noticed that he was looking right at my smile. I wondered if he could read everything my smile was saying.

The other possibility was that he was staring at the red volcano on my chin.

I decided to change the subject.

"What is your middle name?"

"Wayne," he answered confidently.

"David Wayne Philips," I said aloud.

We kept talking about our families and school. The time passed quickly and it seemed like we were old friends.

When we arrived at the canoe livery and assembled for our instructions, we were sent out in pairs. Kadie and I paired up.

"Don't you dare drop your paddle," Kadie joked.

"I think we're in trouble," I pointed. We both looked out at the river and noticed it was much wavier than Hazy Lake. We climbed into the canoe and waited for our turn to go. When it was our turn, we dug our paddles into the sand and pushed off, the way the instructors had told us. Soon we were on our way, straight down the river. There were canoes in front and in back of us.

I was well aware of David and Kevin's canoe two spots behind. Before we knew it, they were next to us and bragging about their sweet skills. We were not interested in letting them move ahead. So we paddled until our arms felt like spaghetti. I looked at Kadie and could tell she was worn out too.

We noticed the sky was getting dark and it was

not even noon. Kadie was the first to fully realize, "I think it's gonna rain."

"I think you're right," I said, unable to hide my excitement. Mrs. Hebner was in a canoe with her husband behind us. I wondered if she had planned to have a relaxing boat ride.

The rain soaked us in a moment. It was that smooth warm kind of rain that hugs you all over. We looked to the shore for help. The guides motioned for us to keep paddling.

It came down so hard it began to fill our canoe. The problem was that we were supposed to canoe a mile downstream to the other building where there was a cafeteria and gift shop.

Kadie and I laughed uncontrollably and then took a collective deep breath. We had forgotten how tired we felt and we just wanted to get this canoe to the stop before it sank.

"Let's stop paddling and try to get some of this water out of the boat," Kadie suggested. The water rushed so fast that the boat kept moving on its own. Our main concern now was that the canoe wanted to tip over. We used our hands as cups and splashed water out of the wobbling canoe. I looked over to see how the boys were doing. They looked as desperate as we did but they were moving past our canoe. We tried to catch up; it was all so fun and exciting!

Kevin and David reached the embankment just before us. They stopped to help us safely to shore. I noticed what a gentleman David was and realized he was that way with everyone.

We all headed to the cafeteria where the workers had prepared for our arrival. They ushered us into the bathroom and handed us a towel on the way. They were eager to let us know they sold dry tee shirts in the gift shop. I told Kadie she could stay in the bathroom while I found us dry shirts. She gratefully handed me a wet five-dollar bill.

David was in the gift shop looking for a shirt. He picked one quickly. I grabbed two light green shirts with pretty pine trees.

"Do you want to sit with me on the way home?" he asked.

"Sure," I agreed. I realized that my hair was all wet. I wondered if I looked like a boy. Sometimes, wet hair made me look kind of dudeish.

"I'll see you on the bus," I said as I finished paying for the shirts. Why did it seem like David was so much better than me at this crush thing?

When I got to the bathroom I gave Kadie her shirt and changed mine. Then I inspected myself in the mirror. Bonnie was next to me. She was much more prepared. She had a small bag with lip-gloss, a comb and hair spray to freshen up.

She must have noticed me desperately combing through my hair with my fingers, because she informed me that my hair was a huge mess.

I assumed she was being a jerk, but then she picked up her comb and hairspray and headed toward my messy hair.

In two minutes, she had it looking better than it had looked in months.

On the way home Davey and I talked about our families some more and I was feeling so comfortable I decided it was time to ask him about Cecelia.

"Did you know that the baker who is in prison for murdering your aunt used to live in my house?" I began carefully.

"Actually, I did know that."

"We didn't know anything about the murder when we moved in." I let him know.

Suddenly, I wanted to tell David about the letters. It seemed like he had a right to know.

"My mom doesn't talk about Aunt Cecelia very much, but she did tell my dad about a family moving in to the baker's house and then when you came to class and talked about living on the lake, I figured it was your family."

"Does your mom still get sad about her sister?" I probed.

"We don't bring up Aunt Cecelia or the baker in our family. She cries every year on Aunt Cecelia's birthday."

"I know some things about your aunt because I found letters in the house," I stopped and looked at David.

"Are you serious?" David wrinkled his nose and waited.

"Do you want to see them?" I asked. I waited a

few seconds and then changed my mind. "How about if I bring you the letters tomorrow and you can decide what to do?"

He agreed to my plan. After all, there were only three days of 6th grade left.

On Thursday, I brought the letters from Cecelia and lunches for me and David. My plan was to hide out in the library during lunch.

We sat at the small table behind the history books. I handed him his brown paper sack and whispered in my most mysterious voice, "One night I found a hole in the floor of my closet. Inside were letters to the baker, Arne. Some of the letters were from your aunt Cecelia. I didn't figure out that Cecelia was your aunt until later, but the letters made me very curious."

I handed David the letters and sat silently as he read. His face was full of doubt.

I started talking again, "Did you know that some people in town think the baker is innocent? And did you know that the trial was done really quickly even though they never found your aunt's b...?" I stopped suddenly because I could see that I'd gone way too far. I forgot for a minute that this was not just a mystery to David. This was his family.

"Arne, killed my aunt on April 25th, 1960. My mom is sure of it. She hates it when people say they think it was someone else. He thought that if he couldn't marry her, then no one could. These letters were probably put in the closet to make the baker seem innocent. I bet this isn't even my aunt's handwriting."

David looked hurt and angry. I felt terrible. "I'm sorry." I mumbled as he walked out of the library leaving his lunch behind. I wondered if he'd ever forgive me.

I knew that date sounded very familiar.

Chapter 13

SUMMER BREAK BEGINS

"But I tell you, love your enemies and pray for those who persecute you." Matthew 5:44 (NLT)

The day school let out, everyone was talking about the town's Cheese Festival. Dad called it the Cheesy Festival all week. But, just to quiet our constant begging, he took us. As we drove up, the aroma of fried cheese filled the air. The fresh, green, fields were filled with busy people, signs painted in oranges and yellows, a ferris wheel and bright red barns. This was the perfect start to summer.

As we stepped through the gate, a man wearing a cowboy hat ran up to Dad asking if he knew how to milk a cow. My dad reluctantly nodded his head and admitted he had spent a summer in high school working on a dairy farm. The insistent man eagerly led him to a barn where everyone talked him in to signing up for the race. It sounded simple enough, the first team to fill a cup with milk won a trophy and their picture would be posted in the town hall. I figured it was a relay race.

With an hour until the race, Mom gave Carrie and I each five dollars and the chance to spend it with our friends. I found Kadie at the cheesecake bakeoff where she had just won second prize for her chocolate cheesecake.

With a beautiful red ribbon around her neck, she led me to the barns full of animals raised by kids.

First, we went to the poultry barn where I met Kadie's sassy chicken named Lily.

Then we stepped inside the sheep and goat barn just in time to catch a, not so smiley, Mr. Hill swinging his foot into the side of an innocent sheep. The sheep let out a gut wrenching noise.

"Any kid of mine should do better than fourth place" the angry man yelled at a boy my age before he walked out the door.

"The barn is closed for 15 minutes," the boy turned to us and pointed to the sign we had missed as he comforted the hurt animal.

"Let's go get a good spot at the milking race," Kadie shrugged and we left the awkward barn scene.

"Is that Mr. Hill's son?" I asked nosily.

"Yeah, his dad is so mean to him."

As we approached the main arena surrounded by stands full of people, I saw a sign that said, *The Wild Cow Milking Race* and heard an announcer, "The ambulance has arrived and the race will begin in five minutes," he said.

"Mom, what did we talk dad into?" I looked at her wide-eyed.

"I don't know, I'm scared" she admitted.

"Don't worry!" Kadie comforted us. "Your dad has the safest job. The other two guys catch the cow and hold her down while your dad gets the milk. They don't even need the ambulance most years."

Mom hugged little Annika nervously. "Just tell me when it's over," She begged, hiding her face.

"Mommy, the cow is nice. She is a mommy like you." Tilly pointed to the cow with its calf. This was no normal looking cow. It had big horns and it didn't look happy about being trapped in a little box.

I looked around for Dad but couldn't see him.

I did see Mr. Hill talking to Davey's dad. "Oh, we are so gonna beat them!" I jumped up to cheer.

The announcer introduced the first team. Suddenly, the gate opened. A giant stop watch started counting off the seconds as an angry looking beast came out of the shoot and ran a full circle around the arena, bucking, and breathing fire. Davey's dad came running out with Mr. Hill and another man. Mr. Philips grabbed for the rope that hung from the cow's face. He got it and the cow dragged him several yards before losing him. He jumped up and ran for the cow again, but she wasn't interested in playing this game. She turned and ran straight toward all three men who ran left, right and up the fence. The crowd gasped in fear, but the men didn't give up.

As the cow looped around and turned to see if the men had left, they lunged for her again, from all directions, forcing her to choose who to run down. She chose Mr. Hill and ran with her horns aimed to hit him. I covered Bernie and Tilly's eyes. Just in time, Davey's dad grabbed the rope and stopped the cow dead in her tracks. Mr. Hill grabbed her tail and the last man milked the cow. It took less than a minute to fill the cup. They all ran excitedly toward the judge who ended the time at 3 minutes and 20 seconds. The crowd went wild. Mom peaked at us and asked if it was over.

"We haven't even seen dad," said Carrie.

"Oh man. They did good" Kadie grumbled.

"We're gonna win!" I was sure.

"Let's hope your dad is better at milking then you are at basketball" she laughed.

"Ha, ha." I smiled. She wasn't my friend because of my great talents.

The second team took their turn and finished with a time of four minutes and ten seconds. Then a third team beat Mr. Hill at the last minute finishing in 3 minutes and 5 seconds. Kadie was ecstatic. Mr. Hill stomped out of the arena and didn't stop. We watched him start his cheese colored truck with the angry exhaust pipes and peel out of the grassy parking lot. Twice now, I had seen a not so cheesy side to Mr. Hill.

Finally, when Mom didn't think she could

stand it any longer, Dad's team was announced. Out came a fresh angry cow. Mr. Brady and the other man appeared with my dad several feet behind them. Only their cow didn't look quite so angry. It reluctantly bucked a couple times and ran around the arena, but then it slowed down and came to almost a complete halt when Kadie's dad approached. With only forty seconds on the clock, Mr. Brady tied up the cow and gave it a big hug as it sniffed his hair and bent down. The other man reached for the tail and my dad ran to milk the cow, who by this time was sitting down upright with its udders against the ground.

"Get up!" The men yelled, trying to pull the cow up from the ground.

With only fifty-five seconds on the clock, Kadie's dad jumped onto the back of the cow, waking it up to its feet. My dad began the milking but all of the cheering, seemed to encourage the cow and it's rider to put on quite a show. Kadie's dad took off his hat and swung it around as if he was a rodeo rider and the crowd went even more wild. It was just enough of a show to knock the half filled cup out of my father's hand.

With one minute and thirty seconds on the clock, Kadie's dad hopped off the cow and held it firmly, which awoke the cow's sleeping anger. It began to kick against the man who was holding its tail. Dad moved toward the cow's utters a second time as it tried to riggle away.

It turned its hind legs, kicking once toward dad.

"That cow is getting daddy!" yelled Tilly. She fought mom's hand as she reached to cover her eyes. Everyone could hear our high pitched screams of terror. But, as if it was tired again, the cow stopped suddenly and bent down to sniff the dirt. All three guys jumped into action, doing their job perfectly.

With two minutes and thirty seconds on the clock, my dad and his new teammates all ran toward the judges with the cow chasing them. Hopping the fence, they sprawled out on the grass, exhausted, as their families ran to congratulate the champions of this crazy race. My mom was the first to arrive, kissing my dad's face and apologizing.

"I'm getting too old for this" said Kadie's dad as his family helped him off the ground and cheered.

As we celebrated, I noticed Davey in the crowd

"That's your dad?" he pointed.

"Yep."

"Cool" he nodded and kept walking.

Your dad did good too!" I yelled, hoping this meant I was forgiven.

My dad beamed as we walked away that evening. In one hand he held my mom's hand and in the other he held a trophy. I was sure I would never hear him call it the Cheesy Festival again.

For the summer, my mom was babysitting one of the neighbor kids while his mom was at work three days a week. His name was Ryan and he was Tilly's age. It was strange having a four year old boy around the house. He could turn anything into a car, a road, or a mountain.

Carrie and I were allowed to ride in to town on our bikes. A couple of times a week we rode out to an old orchard we had found. The first time we went, we couldn't find anyone around the orchard and no one answered the door at the old house. But we tried again. We really wanted to pick some of the ripe strawberries before it was too late. Carrie knocked twice and we waited. We were surprised when a man who looked to be about sixty answered the door right away.

"What can I do you for?" he asked in a super friendly voice.

"We really like your orchard." Carrie started.

"Yes, and we were wondering if we could buy some of your strawberries," I chimed in handing him two dollars to show we really meant it.

"We've had a bit of a dry spell and I've been under the weather, but you just help yourself to whatever you like," he said.

"Thank you so much," Carrie said gratefully, as we headed toward the strawberries.

We picked as many as we could fit in the front of our tee shirts and rode carefully back home.

Mom was being weird again. She just loved to tease everyone about having a crush on someone. She had already started teasing Tilly about having a crush on Ryan and Tilly was starting to believe it. She followed Ryan around like a little puppy and giggled too much. I rolled my eyes in Mom's direction and she saw me. "Don't roll your eyes at me," she said.

While we were on the back porch eating lunch we noticed Jeff, Ryan's older brother out swimming with a friend. Jeff was in the grade ahead of me and his friend looked like that poor sheep raising heir to the Cheese Soda dynasty. I couldn't believe they were swimming in that gooey water.

After lunch, Carrie and I got to stay up while the other kids took a nap. As we cleaned up from lunch, Mom suddenly yelled, "Maggie, watch the kids, I'll be back." We heard the screen door slam and jumped up to see what was going on. There were some men in a row boat near the shore. Two were pulling someone into the boat and the other was frantically pulling the boat to shore while he yelled and waved one arm at my mom.

"Call 9-1-1!" The man yelled.

Mom turned toward us and yelled for me to call 9-1-1.

"What's your emergency." I heard on the other end of the line. It felt unreal as I explained the best I could what I was seeing outside of our screen door. The boy was on the shore now. Mom was breathing into his mouth like I had seen people do in movies. As I hung up the phone and waited to hear sirens, Carrie grabbed my hand.

He wasn't moving. "Oh, I hope he's not dead," Carrie and I started to panic.

Carrie said, "Let's pray!" so we urgently talked to God as we kept our eyes on our mom. The boy, who looked like Mr. Hill's son, continued to lie still for at least a minute, but Mom kept pumping his chest, listening and breathing into his mouth. Suddenly, the boy popped up and spit out a bunch of water. He slumped over and within minutes an ambulance arrived. Mom came home. We could hardly believe we had watched our mom save a boy's life. She was shaking as she told us that the boys were drunk. The fisherman saw the boy, whose name was Roy Hill, start to drown. She couldn't believe that seventh grade boys were getting drunk.

Chapter 14

FINALLY A LEAD

"Oh, how great are God's riches and wisdom and knowledge! How impossible it is for us to understand his decisions and his ways!" Romans 11:33 (NIV)

Carrie and I continued to ride our bikes every chance we found. We went back to the orchard several times during the summer and learned that the owner's name was Mr. Lester. He retired from a factory in Minnesota and moved back to the orchard, because it was where he grew up.

"We live in the house where the old baker lived," I told him, hoping he would take the bait and tell us what he knew about Arne.

"Oh, the baker" Mr. Lester said with a nod. "Arne's life has been anything but a bowl a cherries."

"What do you mean?" I asked.

"It's been a month of Sundays since I've thought of Arne. Poor guy came to Hillcrest after World War II. He is German and a former Nazi. But, he couldn't change his past and all of that was water under the bridge. In fact, Arne turned against Hitler and all that Nazi garbage, and he helped the good side. The United States let him hide out here in Wisconsin after the war. He set up the bakery here and the people loved his bread and pies but he never completely fit in. Then, when that girl came up missing, people wanted to pin it on Arne. I'd give my right arm to know what really happened on that night. It'd be a crying shame, if he went to prison for nuthin'."

"That would stink," agreed Carrie.

"I had moved to Minnesota by the time Cecelia was murdered, but my mom always kept tabs on everyone in town for me. Arne bought all of his fruit from this orchard. His secretary, Mauve Miller, is one of my sister's best friends."

"Where is Mrs. Miller now?" I asked, hoping she lived nearby.

"Oh, she lives in town and mostly keeps to

herself. She does play the organ at St. Luke's Church every Sunday. *Wowee*! it's hotter than grandma's skillet out here." Mr. Lester wiped his forehead with a handkerchief he pulled from his pocket. "I need me a cheese soda! Can I get you girls one too?"

"Sure, thanks" I said, surprised at how good it sounded. Carrie shook her head and made a face.

As we rode away from the orchard, Carrie was full of questions. I filled her in on everything except the letters. Only David knew about the letters and that was a mistake. I told Carrie that I thought Arne was innocent, but she'd never understand why unless I showed her the letters.

I found Mrs. Miller's phone number and address in our little town phone book without trouble. When I called her, Mauve said she'd be glad to meet with me and tell me about Arne.

Carrie agreed to go with me on my secret mission. She called me a little loony, but she still came. Mrs. Miller was a spunky older lady who insisted we call her Miss. Mauve. She had been a widow for forty-four years. Her husband died in what she called, The Battle of the Bulge on his second tour during World War II. She was pregnant with their son at the time.

When Arne came to live in the town, at first she didn't like the idea of being friendly with a German and former Nazi, but then on January 10, 1949 the day of the fifth anniversary of her husband's death, Arne sent her a card expressing his sympathy and a dozen delicious strudel pastries. She was completely shocked. She said, since she was a Christian, she realized that she had been refusing to forgive the entire country of Germany for what happened to her husband. She said that God reminded her of the verse in Matthew that tells us we should love our enemies and she was finally ready to forgive.

I looked over at Carrie and could see that she was feeling as emotional as me.

She continued, "I went into the bakery the next week and asked him why he made such a gesture. He said he prayed that all people would heal from the horrors of that dreadful time in history. Then he offered me a job as secretary. He and I became friends. He understood that my heart would always belong to my dear Walter and I understood that he missed his family in Germany, desperately.

"During Arne's trial, I was there every day," she went on, "but Arne's lawyer never called me as a witness. I wanted to stand up in that courtroom and proclaim Arne's innocence, but I never had a chance. I guess he did it to protect me. Arne would never have laid a finger on that dear sweet girl."

"What about Mr. Hill?" I jumped in with an accusing tone.

Miss. Mauve chuckled at the mention of the name, "You mean the maker of that dreadful soda? He used to come in the bakery a lot. I think he had a thing for Cecelia. He came in the bakery early on the day of the murder, but he had twenty witnesses. They all said Fletcher was in the Columbus library working from 11:00 in the morning until it closed at 9:00 pm. The fisherman found Arne's empty canoe around 8:00 that night. Fletcher Hill is cheesy, but I don't think he's a killer either."

"Could he have paid someone to do it?" I suggested.

"This was before cheese soda. Mr. Hill had no money back then."

Hmmm. Mauve saw my disappointment and tried to console me. "I have every piece of information from the courtroom and the newspapers and I haven't been able to make a bit of sense of this for thirty years.

I hate to disappoint you, but this case is as cold as my arthritic hands."

Carrie and I smiled and tried to keep from laughing while Miss. Mauve pulled out the binder full of information from the trial. I told her I was interested in the picture of the canoe. When she handed me a copy of the photo, I saw a jacket, a book, a thermos, and a plate with two strudels neatly lying inside the canoe. There were two strudels on a plate. I was pretty sure Cecelia had never been in that canoe.

"What is *Dr. Jekyll and Mr. Hyde*?" I asked Miss. Mauve because I noticed the title of the book in the canoe.

It's about a man who changes back and forth from being kind to being violent and awful.

"Could Arne have been that way?"

"I am certain that Arne is not a Mr. Hyde but the book had been checked out under Arne's name."

"So it was probably a set-up." I decided aloud.

"Has anyone considered that Cecelia may have tried to go swimming in Hazy Lake and gotten stuck in all of the muck," Carrie suggested. "The bottom of that lake is like quick sand."

Miss. Mauve and I shrugged our shoulders as we all stared out the window, looking for the answer.

"The Lord is faithful. His ways are mysterious. He allows people to make horrible choices on this earth, but He always has a plan for His people." Miss. Mauve continued, "When I have visited Arne in prison, I have been surprised that his faith in Jesus has grown even stronger. He reads the Bible every day. He has not lost hope and he shares his hope with other prisoners. He knows that no matter what happens on this earth, he will spend eternity in heaven. Still, I hate to think of him in prison. I pray for his innocence to be made known."

We left Miss. Mauve's house with hard candy in our pockets and a new friend, but no idea who killed Cecelia. I was overwhelmed with the feeling that we would never know the answer. Even worse was the feeling that Arne was alone in prison, innocent. Could Arne really be close to God after being accused of murder and spending thirty years in jail?

Chapter 15

A LITTLE BIT OF WEIRDNESS

"Give all your worries and cares to God, for he cares about you" 1 Peter 5:7 (NLT).

Near the end of summer, my parents decided to leave all of us girls on our own while they went out for a date. I was officially twelve now and Carrie was almost eleven. We could call the neighbors if anything went terribly wrong. Our parents hadn't been on a single date since we moved to Wisconsin so we were happy to help.

They were gone less than a half hour when my dad came in, alone, obviously upset, and slammed the door. "Your mother is going to make me lose all of my hair before I'm 40," he said.

"Where is she? What happened?" We asked. "We were arguing and she jumped right out of the van while I was driving," he explained. "I must have been going twenty-five miles an hour and she just jumped out," he finished in a bewildered tone.

"Is she okay?" we all wanted to know.

"Oh yeah, she's fine, but she wouldn't get back in the car," he said as he walked toward his room. Bernice began to cry.

"She'll be back soon. Don't go out looking for her. She just needs some time to cool down," he tried to reassure us. He tucked Annika into bed and then said, "I'm going to lie down."

The rest of us stayed up and tried not to imagine mom getting lost on her way around the lake. Carrie and I tried to comfort Bernice and Tilly by telling them that everything was going to be okay. "God is with Mommy wherever she is." We all knew that Mom and Dad argued sometimes, but nothing like this had ever happened. We decided to pray and go to bed.

I pulled out my Bible, wondering what truth God might have to help my troubled heart. I opened to John 15 because it had become my favorite. It all sounded so simple. Stay close to Jesus, and he would take care of everything else. Did it seem like that was true?

I read more of the words of Jesus. In John 14, I read "Do not let your hearts be troubled. You believe in God; believe also in me. My Father's house has many rooms; if that were not so, I would have told you. I am going there to prepare a place for you. And if I go and prepare a place for you, I will come back and take you to be with me that you also may be where I am." There really was so much to look forward to. No matter what happened, I could trust Jesus.

Just as I was falling asleep I heard a *tap-tap* sound. I looked up at the window and saw a figure that looked like my mom standing on the other side of the glass. I stood up and moved to the window because the image looked so real. Suddenly, the tap came again and I heard my mom's muffled voice say, "It's me! Mom!"

"Oh!" I yelped and quickly opened the window to help her in. She was crying and obviously exhausted. She told me a similar story to the one my dad had told and then asked if Dad seemed worried. I told her that he definitely was. She asked where he was and I told her he was in bed.

She looked disappointed and told me she was going to sleep on the couch in the basement. I went down with her and helped make a bed on the couch with the funny feeling that for one strange night, I was the mom. It was all very weird and I hoped that everything would be back to normal in the morning. I wondered if fights like this were what caused people to get divorced. I started to let the worrying take over, but all at once God reminded me that this was something I couldn't fix.

A few days later, Mom gathered everyone together and announced. "I'm pregnant!" We were excited but also aware that six kids meant we would be in a completely new family category. Six kids means your family is so big that when you walk into a restaurant or store, everyone stops what they're doing for a minute to comment.

There was fresh excitement in our family and we were all happy. For the next few days everyone was asking our dad if he hoped for a boy this time. He'd say, "either one is fine with me." But I wondered too if he would finally like to have a son in the family to balance out all of the girl stuff.

One day, not long after Mom had given us the news, on the way to the mall to get new school shoes,

Dad seemed to be in an extra good mood. He really liked babies. He turned to Mom and said, with a smile and nudge, "Now I know why you jumped out of the van the other day. You always get a little crazy when you're first pregnant. I'm just glad you didn't get hurt." My sisters and I all watched the blood rush to Mom's head and breathed a sigh of relief when she didn't jump.

At the mall, there was a modeling agency looking for fresh talent. When they saw Bernice, they walked up and talked to our parents excitedly. Our parents weren't interested, but Bernice suddenly became aware of her modeling instincts.

Ever since she was a baby, Bernice had been photogenic. People raved about her beautiful puppy dog eyes and cheekbones. Usually it didn't make me jealous, because she really did have beautiful eyes. But, after the mall incident, for a whole week, Bernice did nothing but practice walking down an imaginary runway with a book on her head. We even caught her doing a kissy face in the mirror.

Bernice's runway walking inspired Mom to organize a fashion show for the whole family. Mom and Dad were the audience. We each put on our favorite outfit and took our turn walking the runway.

Mom even made us brownies with grape juice. Tilly picked out the most colorful and fun outfit. We all decided she would one day be a fashion designer and Bernice got her modeling moment after all!

Chapter 16

MR. OLINGER

"The words of the reckless pierce like swords, but the tongue of the wise brings healing." Proverbs 12:18 (NIV)

Summer soon came to an end, school started and I was officially in junior high. I now had a locker and a lot more homework. We learned to play volleyball in gym and I heard that cheerleading tryouts were taking place in a couple of months. The best part was that David sat right in front of me and he was not mad at me anymore. In fact, he did not bring up his aunt at all.

At lunch, I spotted Roy and before I gave it a second thought I yelled. "Hey, Roy Hill, my mom saved your life this summer." Roy came toward me with the same expression as the day when his dad kicked his sheep. I had embarrassed him.

"Can you just let that go, please?" he asked. "It's all I heard about all summer."

"Sorry, I shouldn't have said anything. I can let it go," I agreed.

"That's all right, I'm used to it. Hey, you live in that murderer's house, don't you?" Roy inquired.

"Actually, I don't think the baker is a murderer and I've spent quite a bit of time trying to figure out who did," I smiled with satisfaction.

"What! You're crazy! Before that lunatic killed Cecelia, my dad planned to marry her."

"I'm sure he did." I said and then slapped my hand to my mouth, but not soon enough.

"Wait a minute. Do you think you're some kind of a little kid detective? Do you think my dad murdered that girl?" Roy seemed to read my mind.

He looked at me with wide-eyed disgust and continued, "You do. You think my dad murdered her and now you're trying to be my friend or something."

I watched him walk away and regretted the whole conversation. I knew I had made a mistake. I determined that I needed to get a better hold on my tongue. It was going to be difficult. For a shy girl, I had a big mouth. I asked God to change me and help me fix my tongue problem.

After lunch, was math class. My math and social studies teacher was Mr. Olinger. Mr. O was a tall man in his fifties who didn't smile much. His room was covered in posters that said things like, "Sleep at your own risk!" and "$5 charge for whining!"

He was a good teacher but there was one problem with Mr. O that I couldn't get past. Mr. O was the only person in the entire school who my parents really knew, because he was part of our church. The reason this was a problem was simple: my mother finally had a spy to fill her in on what I did all day.

Mr. O found out quickly about my big mouth problem when he told the class, "Almost everyone has an arm span that is equal to their height." Right away that sounded completely impossible to me. I wrinkled my eyebrows in disapproval and shook my head just a tiny bit.

He saw my expression and spoke up, "There's

someone who doesn't believe me."

I felt confident I was right so I plainly stated, "No way, my arm span is not nearly as long as my height." Mr. Olinger was happy to prove me wrong and instructed me to come up to the front of the class so that he could compare my arm span to my height. When he did, to my amazement, my arm span was within a half inch of my height.

I walked back to my desk, deflated.

"I didn't think he was right either." David turned and whispered.

Before bed, I pulled out the letters once again. It was useless, I practically had them memorized, but Roy sounded so sure. Like he knew something I didn't.

That's when I saw it! A tiny napkin folded carefully and hidden in the corner of the space under the floor.

April 26, 1960- Arne

She, my heart

I, her heart bearer
Truth so clear,
I know, but it is unknown
Evil exists in this world,
I have seen it
Never wanted it to reach her,
I'm afraid I led her to it.
Lord, help me undo, what
I have done.

The poem was so beautiful but so sad. What did it mean? Had Arne led her to something that hurt her? Was this a confession poem?

On Wednesday, everyone was talking about the homecoming dance. When we were finished with our Social Studies assignment David turned around to chat. He got right to the point. I could hardly believe the words that were coming out of his mouth when he asked, "Do you want to come with me to the dance?"

"Yes" I answered and I heard my voice sounding so sure, but I wondered what my mom and dad would say.

"They have dances for seventh grade students?" Dad asked, in disbelief, later that evening. He made it sound like we were preschoolers. "I've never heard of dances for seventh grade," he continued. "When I was in school, we only had dances for high school and that was enough."

I realized this was not going well and decided to chime in. "David is a nice boy Dad and I really like him." I tried to assure. I don't think it helped, because within a minute my dad had made up his mind.

"My answer is no, and that's final. Don't even try to argue."

Now I was stuck. What was I going to tell David? It was so embarrassing that my parents thought I was too young. Why didn't they trust me?

The next day Kevin asked Kadie to the dance and I ended up telling David the humiliating truth. He just looked confused, but that would soon be the least of my worries.

Later that day in math class, I was trying to listen but started to doodle instead. I figured Mr. O. would think I was taking notes. Without thinking, I had written, "I love David," with a heart around it on my paper. I panicked while maintaining an outward calmness, scribbled over it lightly, then ripped it out of my notebook slowly and carefully. I hid the page safely under my math book and looked for an opportunity to throw it away before David saw it.

We finished math and headed straight to typing class. I liked typing because it was one thing I did well. When I was eight, my dad got Carrie and me a typing game. It was a little keyboard with a screen, kind of like a calculator. As the words moved by we typed them and it timed us and gave us a score. For Carrie and I it was a big competition.

When we got back to class, Mr. Olinger was standing in front of us with a piece of paper in his hand. He looked very serious and I knew someone was about to get in trouble.

Suddenly, the page he was holding flipped ever so slightly and I realized what he had in his hand. It was my mindless doodle from math class. What in the world was he doing with it? He held it up for everyone to read and, of course, everyone started talking and giggling when they read it. A few students looked over at me and I was pretty sure that my face was even whiter than usual. Bonnie looked very pleased. Mr. Olinger looked directly into my eyes and said, "This is not appropriate for school. Did you write this Maggie?"

I froze, afraid to look at David. Afraid to look at anyone.

Right there, right then, I knew I had a decision to make. Would I tell the truth and take the consequences or would I lie? I knew the right thing to do.

"No," I lied, the lie of a coward, but everyone knew the truth. Right away I felt guilty, but instead of admitting my guilt and telling the truth, I became angry.

Why were my parents and Mr. Olinger trying to sabotage my life? I was just a kid. I knew I wasn't really in love. I really wanted to follow God, but they were making it so hard.

On the night of the dance, I stayed in my room moping. My sisters came in, trying to help me feel better, but I did not want to cheer up. Mom came in and instead of the expected lecture she asked, "Do you understand why your dad said no about the dance?"

"He thinks I'm too young," I repeated his words.

"It's more than that though. Your dad wants to protect your heart and protect you from being in situations that might get your heart into trouble. You have several years of boy drama ahead of you. It's fun, but it can also get confusing and sticky. It's important that you let us help you. It's important that you trust us to help protect you in the boy area."

"He's a nice boy Mom," I countered.

"But what if he had tried to kiss you tonight? What would you have done? Once you have that first kiss, life becomes more complicated," she answered. "I know you want to live for Jesus, so trust me, it's much easier if you keep the boy drama for when you are older and ready to get married. For now, you can focus on friends, school, family, and your relationship with God. I know I tease you about boys, but I told your dad I would try to stop that. For now, you can be friends with boys. Trust us. More importantly, trust God." She showed me a Bible verse about not falling in love too early.

"You don't plan on picking my husband do you?" I smiled. The truth was, my heart didn't know how it could like anyone more than David but, I didn't know if David really loved God and I knew I had a lot more to learn about real love.

The day after the dance, Kadie informed me

that most of the seventh graders didn't have any date and everyone took turns dancing with everyone else. She said I probably had more fun at home.

"Those dresses are really uncomfortable," she said.

I could tell she was trying to make me feel better, and it worked.

A few days later, we got our report cards in the mail. Mom handed me mine with a look of concern. There were 3 A's, 3 B's and a C- in math. My heart sank. It was my first C ever. I had been spending too much time day dreaming about David and the Arne mystery.

"I'll work harder in math," I promised my mom. "I do get distracted sometimes and math is harder this year. Sometimes I forget to bring the homework home from school and I don't get it done." I slipped away to my room for some alone time.

"Maggie, get your math homework done and then come clean the living room," my mom called as I walked down the hall.

It took an hour to figure out the first fifteen math problems. Doing homework the right way took so long. Proving Arne's innocence seemed so much more important but after finding the poem, I wasn't so sure anymore.

Chapter 17

REGIFT

"People who conceal their sins will not prosper, but if they confess and turn from them, they will receive mercy."
Proverbs 28:13 (NLT)

Bonnie invited me to her slumber party one Friday night. We were going to go to the football game and then back to her house.

"Are you ready Maggie?" Mom yelled and I suddenly realized I didn't get a gift. I searched my room for something I could re-gift. In my jewelry box I found a pair of cute earrings I had never worn. The only other thing I could find to go with it was my cute red hair scrunchie with the scarf pattern. I knew Bonnie would like it because it matched our school colors. The only problem was she had seen me wear it.

"Maggie, if you want to go to this party, we

need to leave in five minutes," Mom yelled.

I decided to give Bonnie the earrings and the scrunchie. Then convinced my mom to stop at the soda shop on the way where I found cream cheese Chap Stick to complete the gift.

The first thing all of us did was go to Bonnie's room and dress up for the football game. Bonnie's room was not very big, but it was completely covered in posters. There was a picture of every famous teenager I could think of: Johnny Depp, Michael J. Fox, Winona Ryder and more that I didn't even recognize.

I put on more makeup then I had ever worn and looked in the mirror, wondering if I looked any better.

The sun went down, as we walked to the game. Hillcrest was winning, but we weren't paying much attention. Instead, we stood around in a circle talking and looking for people we knew.

I didn't see David until half time. When he walked by, I wondered if he thought I looked ridiculous. Suddenly, my knees gave out. I whipped my head around in time to see David and some of his friends running away laughing. The awkwardness of trying to be a teenager was broken and we ran after them to get our revenge. We played tag for the rest of the game.

When it was over, all of the girls went back to Bonnie's house for cake and gift opening. Bonnie got a Whitney Houston tape, a colorful picture frame that looked like a high heel shoe, and some more posters for her wall. She opened my gift last.

She seemed to like the earrings, but took one look at the scrunchie and said, "I've, most definitely seen you wear this scrunchie," with a disgusted look on her face.

Once again, I was stuck between a lie and total embarrassment. "It's a different one." I lied.

Immediately, I felt ashamed. I'm pretty sure she knew the truth and everybody else did too. They would probably be watching to see if I wore my scrunchie and I never would again, because Bonnie had it in her pile of gifts.

Why did I lie anyway? I asked myself. The truth would not have been so bad. Maybe if I told her the truth she would have felt honored instead of disgusted. But, now it seemed like it was too late. I would have to admit to everyone that I was a liar and a cheap gift giver. Why did I lie?

As we went to sleep, we watched a movie about a girl who was searching for a prom date. Maybe my mom was right. The girl in the movie didn't care about anything, but boys.

When I got home the next day, I slept in until two. Mom and Dad sent us downstairs to play until dinner, but we were cold. We started to sneak upstairs. Carrie climbed to the top of the stairs and motioned for us to be quiet. We all focused on what they were saying and realized they sounded worried.

"I can get a job waitressing on the weekends," Mom said. Then, they brought up the word that could change everything: move.

We motioned for Tilly and Annika to go back down stairs with us.

"But I'm cold," whined Tilly. Carrie handed her a blanket and we snuggled on the couch to discuss what we had just heard.

We agreed that we did not want to move back to Michigan. We made a pinky pact to be on our best behavior and try to help Mom and Dad as much as possible.

After a few days, it all seemed to blow over. Mom and Dad didn't bring up the four-letter M-word and we didn't bring it up either.

It was time for cheerleading. Mom said I could try out. She told me not to get my hopes up. She said that my loud voice was the biggest thing I had going for me. She wasn't saying it to be mean. My lack of grace was a family joke.

Before tryouts, we practiced the cheers for two weeks. My favorite cheer involved introducing the cheerleader next to me. It went "one-two-three-four-five, my pirates don't take no jive. Say-a, six-seven-eight-nine-ten. Back it up and meet my friend."

After three nights of tryouts, the coaches were going to announce who made the squad. We all stood in a line, facing the judges, waiting for our fate to be announced.

The coach began by saying, "We wish we could choose all of you." Then she paused and turned to pick up a piece of paper from in front of one of the other judges. "The B team this year will consist of: Norah Roberts, Megan Wallace, Michelle Mills, Melissa

Rodgers, Bonnie Raven and Maggie Pierce." I was shocked to hear my name.

I turned to the girls who didn't make the team and gave each of them hugs. They didn't seem too sad and I was relieved. After they left to call for rides, the rest of us were given papers with all of the information we needed for the season.

When we arrived to our first game, we were led to the girl's locker room. We all inspected ourselves carefully in the mirror. I noticed for the first time that my eyebrows were growing out of control. How long had they been like that?

An older girl, who I thought was Roy's girlfriend stood next to me, "Aren't you the girl who thinks Roy's dad killed Cecelia Walsh?" she asked.

"I'm just trying to figure out who did." I forgot about my eyebrows and the big crowd of people I was about to stand in front of and began to wonder who else knew about my big mouth.

Bonnie came in with a smirk on her face, pointing at her hair, "Does my scrunchie look familiar? Where's yours?"

"I lied okay. I don't know why I lied. I'm

sorry. It was my favorite and I thought you would like it." I surprised myself with my confession.

Bonnie looked shocked and must have been speechless because she just mumbled, "It's cool," and walked away.

After the basketball team came out, we stepped on the gym floor and introduced each other. Mr. Hill sat in the stands and I thought I saw him glaring at me.

During half time, I took a walk and tried to hide from Mr. Hill. This was getting sticky.

On my way back, I spotted him. I tried to hide behind the pop machine but it didn't work.

"So, the same girl who wanted me to autograph her jelly bean *beg* is now the girl who's telling people I'm a murderer." he started. "I want you to know what you're saying could get you into a lot of trouble young lady."

"I'm sorry; I didn't tell anyone I think you did it. I'm just trying to…"

"Be careful what you say!" He interrupted, in an angry voice. "I would never have laid a finger on Cecelia. That's all you need to know."

He was angry.

Without thinking, I spewed, "I'm just trying to solve the murder and some of the clues point to you. I think you're the one who set up that canoe to make it look like Arne was the killer. It fits perfectly. You worked at the library so it was easy for you to check out *Dr. Jekyll and Mr. Hyde* in Arne's name." I gasped, realizing I had said too much.

He stepped back in shock and looked around to see if anyone had been listening. I decided to book it back to the gym. How could I be such a chicken and have such a big mouth?

Our team won, but my heart did not calm down. Every time we stepped out to face the audience and cheer, it was Mr. Hill's face I saw, giving me an intimidating glare. David played really well but I was so distracted I didn't get a chance to tell him. I might be risking my life if I came to another game. This was getting scary.

It was late when I got home, but Mom was wide-awake with something to tell me. The Berlin Wall was being torn down. I ran to the television because I could hardly believe it. I wondered what made those leaders change their mind. On ABC news we heard

Peter Jennings say, "the wall doesn't mean anything anymore." I wondered if this meant all of those people could go see their family and friends who were on the other side of the wall.

I went to bed feeling so many emotions, all at once. I felt relief for the people of Germany but a new fear for my own safety.

I needed to solve the mystery as soon as possible. If Mr. Hill was a murderer, I was in danger. If he wasn't, I was a jerk. No more distractions. I grabbed a pen and decided it was time to get organized. I made a timeline of everything I knew about Cecelia and Arne from World War 2 to the coming down of the Berlin Wall. The timeline was loaded with quite a bit of information. It was enough to impress Mr. Olinger, but he would never see this bit of history. Where could I find more? Afraid I had exhausted all of my sources, I pulled out the copy of the newspaper article with the name of Arnie's attorney on it. The name was Ralph Morrison and even though it had been thirty years, I found him easily in the Columbus yellow pages. I planned to call the next day and tell him what I knew. I had to get in touch with Arne's brother or even Arne. But I needed to ask God for help each step of the way because I knew this was too big for me.

Chapter 18

TIME FOR A VERDICT

Yet the Lord longs to be gracious to you; therefore he will rise up to show you compassion. For the Lord is a God of justice. Blessed are all who wait for him!"
Isaiah 30:18 (NIV)

The next day, there was more exciting Berlin Wall news. Peter Jennings was in Berlin reporting. We saw thousands of people dancing on top of the wall and hitting it with hammers while the East Berlin police stood by and watched, stone faced and statue still. There was nothing the police could do to stop it. There was cheering and people were crying because they were so happy. A hundred thousand people had gone through the gate to West Germany to find their family and friends.

I remembered to call Arne's lawyer, but all I got

was his answering machine. I called three more times during the week, but no one answered. It was time to leave a message.

I called at three o'clock and said something like, "Mr. Morrison, I know...I mean, I want to help Arne...I don't know him but...if you still work for him...please call me. My name is Maggie Pierce. My phone number is ...

For the next hour I sat by the phone and wrote down exactly what I wanted to ask Mr. Morrison. The phone rang at 4:15.

"This is Ralph Morrison," said the grandfatherly voice. "Am I speaking with Maggie Pierce?"

"Yes, I live in Arne Werfel's old house and I have been doing some research about his case. I saw, in one of the newspaper articles, that you were his lawyer during the trial."

"Yes, you are correct," said the voice.

"Well, I have found some information which leads me to believe that Arne may be innocent."

"Is that so? Well, this is interesting and I am

curious. I'm not terribly surprised."

"Really, why not?" I had to know.

"Some time ago, I learned that Arne's brother, who still lives in Germany, had been trying to sabotage him for years. He had tried to create problems for Arne in America. He wanted Arne to be sent back to Germany where he would probably have been punished for helping the United States during World War 2. Arne's brother is very powerful in the East German government. He might be powerful enough to cover up a murder. In fact, I'm curious about how the Wall's fall has affected old Detlef."

"Really" I showed my interest and hoped Mr. Morrison would continue.

"Arne was very concerned with his brother's welfare and the welfare of his brother's wife and two children. When I found the testimonies of incriminating evidence against Arne's brother, Arne told me to stop investigating."

"Arne wanted to stay in prison?" I asked in disbelief.

"If it meant his brother would get into trouble then Arne did not want me to keep looking. He just wanted to stay in prison."

"Can you give me Detlef's address?" I asked and hoped he'd be impressed. The lawyer told me he had never been able to find the address for Arne's brother. He did know Detlef's wife was, coincidentally, called Zilla which is a German nickname for Cecelia. He told me I should not try to talk to Detlef. Before he hung up, he called Detlef a dangerous dude.

The conversation left me with more questions than ever, one big one in particular. Did Arne's brother commit the ultimate sabotage? Did Arne figure out that Detlef's wife is THE Cecelia? Could Cecelia Walsh be alive?

I imagined Arne in prison, a brave man who was completely stuck. I've got to help him, I thought. I pulled out the poem Arne had written on a napkin. Now, it all made sense. How could I act like everything was fine when I knew an innocent man was in prison?

Within a week, my parents called us all into the living room to talk. Carrie and I gave each other knowing looks, because we were both pretty sure of what our parents were about to say.

"No, I'm not moving!" I jumped in before they

had a chance to tell us. I wanted them to know there was nothing they could say to change my mind, but immediately the Holy Spirit reminded me that I was not the boss.

"Maggie, we know this is going to be hard for all of you girls," Mom started. "But we have thought long and hard about this and your dad and I both think it is the best decision for our family right now."

I nodded, but began to cry, "Why didn't you ask us what we thought before you made the decision?"

"Sometimes, it's better if your mom and I make the big decisions on our own," Dad added in a voice that meant, "this is not open for discussion."

I nodded and wanted to run to my room and slam the door, but God gave me the strength to control myself.

Later, as I tried to fall asleep, the fears got bad again. I kept trying to talk to God, but He seemed so far away. That night, I really cried to Him. I started talking to Him, but then I started to write to Him.

"Why, why, why?" I wrote. "You are God and You can open up the middle of the sea so people can walk through. You can bring dead people to life. You can do anything. Please keep my family in Hillcrest."

But there was only silence. "Why did we move here at all?" I continued anyway. "And why don't I get to make decisions? And worse, why is an innocent man in prison?"

My questions lead me into a restless sleep.

Chapter 19

THE END OF SEVENTH GRADE AS I KNEW IT

"Trust in the LORD with all your heart
and lean not on your own understanding;
in all your ways submit to him, and he will make your paths
straight." Proverbs 3:5-6 (NIV)

On Tuesday night, I pulled out the letters, hoping to find some clue. It seemed like I had reached a dead end. I knew my parents would never let me contact a man who was in prison and I didn't have any way to write to Detlef. He said in the last letter that he was moving.

All of a sudden I had a breakthrough thought, "Oh my goodness, he said he was moving into the family estate! The family estate would have been

Arne's mom's address before she died." I rushed to find the letter from Detlef's mother. I looked on the envelope for a return address. There it was! Was it possible that Detlef was still living in the family estate?

With a month and two days until moving day I completed the letter to Detlef. It was written with words and letters cut out of the newspaper. It said:

DETLEF,

I KNOW CECELIA WALSH IS ALIVE AND YOU HAVE HER. I KNOW THAT THE CANOE WAS A SET UP. YOUR BROTHER HAS BEEN IN PRISON FOR THIRTY YEARS AND HE DID NOTHING WRONG. NOW, YOU WILL GO TO PRISON FOR THE REST OF YOUR LIFE IF YOU DONT SEND HER AND THE KIDS SAFELY TO HILLCREST FOR A VISIT.

I copied the address in Germany from Arne's mother's letter and added six stamps to the envelope, hoping it was enough. Then I dropped the letter into the mailbox at the Piggly Wiggly with no return address and prayed it would work.

Even though God hadn't stopped our move, I knew He was helping me. He was giving me the strength to do things I didn't want to do, things I could not do on my own.

One of the hardest things about moving was telling Kadie, because I knew she was going to be sad too. "My family is moving back to Battle Creek," I forced the words, during lunch.

"Are you serious?" she asked in disbelief.

"I don't want to, but it doesn't matter."

"This is awful!" she moaned.

"I know!" I agreed.

We gave each other a big hug and started to cry a little. It was nice to know she cared so much, but still it was no fun to know we would be split up.

Other people in the cafeteria asked what was wrong and soon everyone in my class knew I was moving. I wondered what David thought.

On the way to the next basketball game I sat in my usual spot near the middle of the bus. As David climbed on, my heart leaped and then fell when I remembered I'd only be seeing him for two more weeks.

I was shocked when he plopped down next to me. I was not prepared for this. He looked at me and asked, "Are you really moving?"

"Yes," I said.

"Do you want to move?" He leaned in closer and I was glad he had asked.

"No, I tried to get my parents to change their mind, but they really want to move. I like it here."

David reached over my way and it took me a second to realize that he was reaching for my hand. I slipped my hand into his and we sat silently.

I held back tears and turned to look out the window. This wasn't the beginning of me and David. This was the end. This was goodbye.

Mom decided that Carrie and I could have slumber parties to spend one last bit of fun with our friends.

Five girls from school came, even Bonnie. Mom rented a movie no one wanted to see so Crystal decided we should start prank calling people's phones. I was hesitant, but we were all in the mood to do something crazy. We decided to prank all of the boys in our class at school. It was ten o'clock and my parents were in their room with the door closed. I think, they thought, we were still safely watching the movie.

We decided we would call Scott first.

"Who can do a good voice?" Kadie asked. We all decided Lena should make the first call. Crystal dialed the number and handed her the phone.

Lena sort of panicked and asked, "What do I say?" Just then a woman who must have been Scott's mom answered the phone.

"Hello, hello?" said the voice on the other end.

"I'm Suzi Howdy-Dudey callin' to twalk to Scott," Lena said in a strong accent from who knows where.

"Okay? It's kind of late, but I'll let you talk to him, for a minute," the lady let out a reluctant chuckle.

Scott got on the phone after a minute and asked, "Who is this?"

"It's Suzi Howdy-Dudey, the girl you met at the skatin' rink last month." Lena said it so smoothly in the same accent and we had to laugh.

We waited for Scott's answer, "I don't know you, you must have the wrong number," he said finally.

"Oh, I know you. You are good-looking Scotty Wileman. You have spiky hair and big muscles."

We heard Scott saying to someone else, "Come listen to this girl, she knows what I look like, but I've never heard of her." We all rolled on the floor laughing as Lena hung up the phone.

"Now let's call D-A-Vid," Lena said and she looked at me. She handed me the phone, but she probably already knew I was too chicken.

Crystal dialed and Kadie agreed to take the phone.

A woman said, "Hello," in an excited voice. Kadie told her something about being an NBA scout and wanting to talk to David.

But the woman cut her off, "He can't talk now, I'm waiting for a call because I just found out my sister is alive!" She hung up the phone and we looked at each other with wrinkled eyebrows.

"Cecelia is alive!! I knew it!!" I yelled with glee.

"Not possible. I think we just got double pranked." assumed Crystal.

The subject changed quickly back to the boys.

"Who should we call next?" Crystal asked. "How about Robby? He'll be funny." Crystal dialed the number, but no one answered. In her frustration, Crystal cursed into the phone.

Immediately, my mom came stomping out of her room. "Girls, I heard what you just said on the other phone and it is time for you all to go to bed," she said in her most angry voice as she turned off the lights and stomped to bed.

There was dead silence and then quiet giggling. Slowly our eyes grew accustomed to the dark.

"Sorry." I felt bad the fun had been cut short. Then I remembered Crystal's reaction and I added to Crystal. "You like Robby, don't you?"

"No!" Crystal denied it. But I had started something and everyone began teasing her.

I reminded everyone to be quiet with a finger to

my lips and a, "*Shhhh!*"

"We have something for you." Crystal changed the subject. She and Kadie surprised me with a gift and a card. I started to cry, as I opened the card and found the nicest notes from my friends. We had a big group hug and I slowly opened the gift.

It was the new *New Kids on the Block* tape. "Whenever you listen to the songs, you can remember us," Kadie gave me a hug.

"Thank you so much. I am not going to forget any of you." I assured them.

Everyone, except me, fell asleep within an hour. I could hardly believe my hunch was right and Cecelia might be alive. How did Arne's brother get Cecelia to marry him? I felt like a real detective. Still, I was exhausted and didn't know if I had the strength to say goodbye to all of these great friends.

In the morning, Crystal and I were the first ones up. Crystal said she felt bad for what she said on the phone. "Your family is so perfect and I feel stupid. I'm afraid to see your mom this morning."

"No, my family is not perfect." I insisted. "Trust me, we have plenty of problems and Jesus is the only

One that makes us different." I noticed Crystal looked interested in what I was saying.

"How can Jesus make you different?" Crystal was clearly not convinced.

"Hmmm, well, my teacher at church always says to start from the beginning. Do you know what sin is?"

"Isn't that when you do bad stuff?"

"Yeah, Adam and Eve started the sin problems when they ate the fruit God had told them not to eat. It meant that sin was a part of the world now and everyone would sin.

"Do you know why sin is a problem? I looked down, feeling a little awkward. I was talking like my teacher always talked.

"God doesn't want us to sin." Crystal looked more comfortable than I did.

"That's true; the Bible says that even one sin has a punishment of death. But when Jesus came, He died for us on the cross. He took our punishment so we wouldn't have to. So, when I asked Jesus to be my Savior, God saw that the payment for my sin had already been paid and He gave me new life. Does that make sense?"

Crystal nodded her head.

"Well, Crystal, if you believe what Jesus said and trust Him, then you can be forgiven too."

"I know I do bad things," said Crystal. "I didn't know that God would forgive me. I thought I had to stop sinning before I could make God happy with me. I just don't know how to do what God wants."

"Wait a minute!" I said excitedly as I ran to grab my Bible.

"Believe me; I know how it feels when you can't seem to do the right thing. I've just been learning to read this on my own and you can too. You can have my copy if you want." I showed her a couple of my favorite verses like John 3:16 and 2 Corinthians 5:21.

"My aunt wants to take me to her church," Crystal admitted. "She'll be happy if I finally say yes."

Just then, Mom walked into the kitchen. "You two need to go back to bed," she insisted. Then she saw the Bible open in front of us. "What are you talking about?" she asked.

"We were talking about sin and about Jesus," I said.

"That's great," said Mom looking at Crystal curiously.

"I'm sorry about what I said last night." said Crystal.

"Believe me, I didn't always know Jesus and I've said my fair share of bad words. I expect a lot from my girls and their friends."

"I'm probably not good enough to be a Christian." Crystal looked at her shoes.

"No, that's not what I mean," said Mom. "Trust me, I sin plenty. I shouldn't have freaked out so much. I'm sorry if I made you feel that way."

"I do want to believe, but I just don't know if I'll be any good at it," said Crystal.

"Jesus called it, being born again when we decide to follow Him. It's like we're a new person and then we grow up again, but this time God's Spirit comes to live in us. You don't need to worry about being good at it. Do you really want to follow Jesus?"

"Yes," Crystal nodded.

"Would you like to start talking to God right now?" asked my mom.

Crystal nodded as she bowed her head and began to pray, "Dear God, I thank you for dying on the cross for my sins. I don't understand why you would do that, but I'm so glad you did. I'm sorry for my sins. Can you make me be born again so I can grow up the right way this time? Thank you for my Aunt Karen and that she has waited all of these years for me to come to church with her." I gave her a hug and my mom wrote a note in Crystal's new Bible.

"You know Crystal?" said my mom. "That spiky hairdo of yours is really growing on me." Crystal and I just laughed and shook our heads.

"I almost forgot! Cecelia might be alive!" I shouted. This is an awesome day!

"If she's been alive all these years, where was she hiding?" Crystal wrinkled her nose.

Chapter 20

CAN IT REALLY BE TRUE?

"For we are God's handiwork, created in Christ Jesus to do good works, which God prepared in advance for us to do." Ephesians 2:10" (NIV)

My family spent all of our free time for the next week packing up the house. It was true that Cecelia was alive. The newspaper and everyone in town were talking about Cecelia being alive and showing up on her sister's doorstep, with two grown daughters, after 30 years.

The cover of the Hillcrest Gazette read:

"Cecelia Walsh is alive. She has returned to Hillcrest, a widow, after thirty years in East Germany. Her late husband was the brother of her suspected murderer, Arne Werfel. Cecelia claims to have been afraid to return until she received a letter from an unknown person in Hillcrest who knew of her whereabouts. Cecelia told us she had no knowledge that Arne Werfel was in prison for her murder. Her disappearance remains under investigation.

Mr. Hill of Hill's Cheese Soda has confessed to obstruction of justice. He has admitted to accepting money in return for setting up the canoe, which served as the material evidence in the conviction of Arne Werfel thirty years ago. Hill received a letter with detailed information about setting up the canoe. After the job he received several thousand dollars. Hill claims to have had no knowledge that the canoe would be used to implicate Arne Werfel for the murder of Cecelia Walsh."

So, Detlef had died! There was a picture of Arne from all of those years ago. It was as if the newspaper report thought they could go back in time. But, I knew that Arne didn't have thick blond hair and a smooth face anymore. He had aged in prison. He may even be sick. Now that he had been proven innocent everyone claimed, "I knew he was innocent." But the only ones I believed were Miss. Mauve, Crystal's mom, and Mr. Lester.

There were two rumors about Cecelia going around and I had no way of knowing which was true. The first was that Cecelia had started dating Detlef while she was a foreign exchange student in Germany and then decided to run away with him. The second was that she was forced to leave Hillcrest when Detlef threatened to hurt her family.

During lunch, David admitted I was right about the letters. He asked me if he could take the letters to his aunt, but I wasn't sure I trusted her. I wanted to ask David so many questions about his aunt, but decided to keep my mouth shut, for a change.

"I think I'm going to leave the letters right where I found them," I told David.

He just shook his head and said, "You're a mysterious girl," which, of course, made me smile.

Crystal had gone to church with her aunt. She was in good hands.

On the night before my last day at school I heard Mom talking on the phone to someone. She said, "I hate to move them to a new school already."

"I know they're resilient," she agreed with whoever was on the phone.

I didn't know what resilient meant. I assumed it meant that kids just bend like a Slinky without ever breaking. Whoever was on the phone, must not have known how badly the bending hurt. I knew my parents felt bad and I knew that other kids had it much worse, but I couldn't stop crying.

I was still in denial. Tomorrow was my last day at Hillcrest school. I was in a fog and none of it felt real. Maybe our van would break down or my dad would be offered an amazing job from one of the ten businesses in Hillcrest. Just in case, I decided to rehearse in my mind how I might say goodbye.

I planned to give Kadie, Lena, Crystal and even Bonnie, big huge hugs. I would assure Kadie that we would be best friends forever, no matter what, and give her the friendship bracelet I made. I would write to her at least once each week.

As I was thinking, I put the best friend necklace from Kadie up over my face and let it sit between my lips. If only I was in charge, I would stay in Hillcrest. I looked at my hands and realized they were clenched tight. I opened them wide and let my palm rest on the bed. I wanted to leave my hands wide open and ready to let God take care of me.

"Lord, I want to trust you." I said aloud.

Still, my little heart hurt.

I turned on my walkman and pressed the play button. The words of *New Kids on the Block* filled my ears, "Please Don't Go Girl" was playing and I imagined David singing it to me. The truth was, David seemed to be just fine.

I turned off the music and put the secret letters into their hiding place one last time. Then I put Cecelia's library book into my bag, knowing I should find a way to put it back. I fell asleep with my palms open and a weird peace about the next day.

Chapter 21

GOODBYE HILLCREST

Consider it pure joy, my brothers and sisters, whenever you face trials of many kinds because you know that the testing of your faith produces perseverance."
James 1:2 (NIV)

By morning, the shaky surreal feeling was back.

When I got into the classroom, I told Mr. Olinger that my parents were coming around 10:30 because they wanted to get through Chicago before rush hour.

I sat through math in a daydream. I was safe because Mr. Olinger wouldn't dare ask me a tough question to see if I was listening.

Within moments of finishing social studies, I realized this was the end. Tomorrow, my class would have a little Christmas party before break and I would be in Michigan. The lake would fill up with fisher-people and we wouldn't be there to skate around them. In the spring, when my class went to camp, I would be sitting in some other classroom.

I felt an enormous snowball of emotions rolling right over me. It hit me first in my face as my lip quivered, followed by uncontrollable tears but it didn't stop there. I could feel my hands shaking and my whole body sort of convulsing. "Are you okay?" Several of my friends rushed to my aid. All I could think was *my heart is breaking*. It wasn't just leaving Kadie and David that hurt, it was the thought of losing my whole known seventh grade life.

"I can't stop crying," I said in frustration as Kadie handed me a tissue for my dripping nose. I tried to take deep breaths and look around. My only goal now was to say goodbye and get out. There nothing else for me to do. I had no other choice but to leave and I might as well do it before I lost complete control of myself.

The only people I said a real goodbye to were Crystal and Kadie. I was too embarrassed to let my tears and runny nose drip all over anyone else. I grabbed my coat and *beg*, stepped out the door of the school with several of my friends, and saw my family's van sitting out front. It was all too much to take in. I turned to my friends one last time and said in a chocked voice, "I really love this place and I will miss you all so much." I walked to the van and opened the door. I gave Kadie one last big hug and turned to wave before hopping in.

Carrie and Bernice were already inside the van. Carrie was crying too. Bernice had a matchbox car from a boy and she said, "Ricky gave it to me and I gave him a kiss on the cheek." I laughed in disbelief. Mom turned and gave us all reassuring looks.

"Guess what?" my dad said with a carefree smile. "We just got an offer on the house. It's from a man named Arne Werfel."

"No way." Everyone knew who Arne was by now.

"It's a generous offer. It's going to take some time to process because Arne has been in prison for so long and there's a whole load of red tape. But, it looks like he's going to get his house back."

My tears of sorrow were now mixed with tears of joy. I was tired and hurting, but also relieved. Bernice looked at me with the saddest eyes. "It's like ripping off a Band-Aid Bernie! We'll be okay. You'll see. It hurts at first, but not for long, and God will be with us Bernie. He always will."

I let Carrie listen to my Walkman because I wanted some time to think and talk to the Great God who I was learning to trust.

So many times I felt stuck, but the truth was, I had hundreds of decisions to make every day. Some of them didn't seem important, like the words I said or how I spent my time, but I was realizing these decisions were more important than I ever knew...

My Heavenly Father and I were getting close. I could see how living for Him and following what the Bible says made life so different. I didn't need to worry so much and no matter what, He had a plan. I was determined to never forget it.

There were so many brave people in this world with problems so much bigger than mine, like the boys in Sudan. Just knowing about their bravery helped me feel stronger.

I looked out the window as we drove past the Hillcrest sign for the last time. I wondered if the town knew we would leave because the sign still said, "Welcome to Hillcrest, The Home of Delicious Cheese Soda, Population 930."

As we moved toward the highway, I looked at the book in my backpack. "Dad, I have a library book in my bag I didn't return. Can we stop at the Columbus library?"

Dad rolled his eyes at me in the rearview mirror but agreed to let me drop off the book. As I walked up the stairs to the library, I saw her.

Cecelia Werfel was walking toward me. It had to be her. She was not very different from the picture in the yearbook. "Cecelia, I think I have what you're looking for," I stepped in front of her.

She stopped suddenly and gasped when I handed her the book. "But how…"

Tears welled up in her eyes and I knew I could trust her. "Don't worry, he knows you didn't want to hurt him."

"I'm the one who found all of the letters Arne kept," I explained as quickly as I could.

"Everything got so messed up. I can't imagine what he went through" Cecelia let the tears drop freely onto the page as she read the words she had hoped Arne would read for all of these years. Suddenly it felt to me like she was twenty years old again. Like they really could get the time back.

"He feels like it was his fault." I remembered the words of the poem and so badly wanted to give her hope.

"Maggie, get back here! We've got to go." Mom yelled.

"I'm actually moving today," I winced and slowly walked back to the van leaving her crying on the steps.

I spent the next hour with a heavy heart, but in my worries God reminded me to turn to Him and I gave Him that burden. This was for Him to handle. Not me.

Two months later, a package came to our new address in Battle Creek. It was from Arne Werfel. Inside was a letter from Arne telling me he had learned from Mauve and his lawyer about how hard I worked to prove his innocence. He thanked me but also assured me that God had been faithful those 30 years in prison. He said God had been faithful in ways he could not explain. At the end, he wrote, "Cecelia thanks you too."

With it, Arne included several delicious strudels but better than that was Arne's Bible from all those years in prison. As I opened it, I saw proof that a person could face huge troubles in this life, but be so filled with faith, hope, and love. That Bible, with its many markings of meaningful history, guided me on toward a closer walk with Jesus.

Extra Activities

Choose a country in the world. See what you can learn about that country. Explore that country with a new set of lenses. Ask God to show you the pain and the needs in that country. Ask God to help you understand the people. Pray for the people. Pray for those who know Jesus and those who don't know Jesus.

Make a timeline of the book starting with the letters and ending with Maggie's move back to Michigan. Highlight the fictional events in one color and then real life events in another.

Discuss differences between the small town middle grade culture then and now.

Can you crack the code of underlined letters from the cover page?

ACKNOWLEDGMENTS

A big thank you to everyone who read this book at its earliest stages. I started this journey with no idea how to self-publish a book. You all have been so gracious: my husband, my kids (Noah, Maggie and Annika), the rest of my great big wonderful family (parents, brothers, sisters, in-laws, a niece, grandma, cousins, aunts and uncles), Aimee, Kenzie and Mazie Shaffer, Viki Rife, Sarah Friddle, Kathie Gerber, Alicia Roberts and Katie Mager. Thank you to my Panera friends for your constant encouragement. Thank you to the Sarah Granville and the Barberton library writers group. What a neat group of writers. Thank you also to Gil Stadler whose editing helped me when I was stuck in a rut. You all gave patient help along the way and I thank you.

ABOUT THE AUTHOR

Katiera grew up in a family of ten where creative juices were always flowing.

She graduated from Grace College and God soon grew in her a passion for helping upper elementary students to draw close to Him and His Word. She wants to write stories that present a picture of middle schoolers who are seeking after Jesus in imperfect but sincere ways. She hopes her 3rd-6th grade readers will grow toward Jesus with their hearts and minds as they read her stories.

She often learns through failure and is so thankful for God's tremendous mercy.

Katiera lives in Ohio with her husband, three kids and pet lizard. They love hiking, learning, making creative messes and seeking to follow Jesus together day by day.

43262366R00109

Made in the USA
Lexington, KY
23 July 2015